r a mo...   say
word.

...e couldn't b...   she
...d so badly wa...   some
...range reason, her throat had suddenly gone raw.

She swallowed, then took a deep breath. "Erik?"
she finally said. "Thank you."

"For holding you?"

"For all of it. But, yes. For this, too."

"What's wrong?" he asked when she started to cry.

"Nothing. Honest," she insisted. "For the first time
in…forever there isn't a thing wrong."

"...en why tears?"

...ause of what you let me feel, she thought. "Be-
...use I'm tired," was easier to admit.

S...e felt his lips against the top of her head. "Then,
...to sleep."

"I don't want to. I don't want to miss you hold-
...me."

"...ou shouldn't say things like that."

"Why not?"

"Because you'll make me forget why I shouldn't
do this," he ... ...shed his mouth
over ...

The ... ...ning

HER HOLIDAY PRINCE CHARMING

BY
CHRISTINE FLYNN

First published in Great Britain 2013
by Mills & Boon, an imprint of Harlequin (UK) Limited,
Eton House, 18-24 Paradise Road, Richmond, Surrey TW9 1SR

© Christine Flynn 2013

ISBN: 978 0 263 90170 2

23-1213

Harlequin (UK) policy is to use papers that are natural, renewable and recyclable products and made from wood grown in sustainable forests. The logging and manufacturing processes conform to the legal environmental regulations of the country of origin.

Printed and bound in Spain
by Blackprint CPI, Barcelona

Christine Flynn admits to being interested in just about everything, which is why she considers herself fortunate to have turned her interest in writing into a career. She feels that a writer gets to explore it all and, to her, exploring relationships—especially the intense, bittersweet or even lighthearted relationships between men and women—is fascinating.

For the lovely ladies
who have made the "Hunt" happen,
and everyone who believes in the fairy tale.

Prologue

"What's on your Christmas list this year? No matter how big or how small, you're sure to find what you're looking for at Seattle's one-stop answer to all your holiday—"

With a quick flick of the dial, Rory silenced the cheerful voice suddenly booming from her car radio. In an attempt to drown out her worries while she waited to pick up her son from kindergarten, she'd turned the music to a decibel she'd never have considered had her five-year-old been in the vehicle.

The ad had just brought to mind the one thing she'd been desperately trying *not* to think about.

She'd hoped to make the holiday special for her little boy this year. Not just special, but after last year's unquestionably awful Christmas, something wonderful. Magical.

As of three days ago, however, she was no longer sure how she would keep a roof over their heads, much less put a tree under it. Due to downsizing, her telecommuting services as a legal transcriptionist for Hayes, Bleaker & Stein were no longer required. She'd needed that job to pay for little things like food and gas and to qualify for a mortgage.

Without a job, she had no hope of buying the little Cape Cod she'd thought so perfect for her and little Tyler. She had no hope of buying or renting any house at all. Since the sale of the beautiful home she'd shared with her husband closed next week, that left her four days to find an apartment and a job that would help her pay for it.

A quick tap ticked on her driver's side window.

Through the foggy glass, a striking blonde wearing studious-looking horn-rimmed glasses and winter-white fur smiled at her. The woman didn't look at all familiar to Rory. Thinking she must be the mom of an older student, since she knew all the moms in the kindergarten class, she lowered her window and smiled back.

Chill air rushed into the car as the woman bent at the waist to make eye contact. "You're Aurora Jo Linfield?"

Rory hesitated. The only time she ever used her full name was on legal documents. And she rarely used Aurora at all. "I am."

"I'm Felicity Granger." Hiking her designer bag higher on her shoulder, she stuck her hand through the open window. The cold mist glittered around her, clung, jewel-like, to her pale, upswept hair. "But please, call me Phil. I'm an associate of Cornelia Hunt. You've heard of Cornelia, haven't you?"

Rory shook the woman's hand, watched her retract it. "I've heard of her," she admitted, wondering what this woman—or the other—could possibly want with her. Nearly everyone in Seattle had heard of Mrs. Hunt, the former Cornelia Fairchild. She'd been the childhood sweetheart of computer genius Harry Hunt, the billionaire founder of software giant HuntCom. Rory recalled hearing of their marriage last summer, even though she'd been struggling within her fractured little world at the time. Media interest in their six-decade relationship had been huge.

"May I help you with something?"

"Oh, I'm here to help you," the woman insisted. "Mr. Hunt heard of your situation—"

Harry Hunt had heard of her? "My situation?"

"About your job loss. And how that affects your ability to purchase another home."

"How does he know that?"

"Through your real estate agent. Mr. Hunt knows the owner of the agency she works for," she explained. "Harry bought a building through him last month for his wife so she'd have a headquarters for her new venture. When he learned why you couldn't move forward with the purchase of the house you'd found, he remembered Mrs. Hunt's project and thought you'd be a perfect referral. So we checked you out." Her smile brightened. "And you are.

"Anyway," she continued, anxious to get to her point. "Cornelia knows of a property for sale that you might want to purchase. She's aware of your current unemployment," she hurried to assure her, "but she said you're not to worry about that little detail right now. Just look at the place. If you're interested, suitable arrangements can be made for you and for the seller.

"It's not exactly what you told your agent you want," she cautioned, reaching into a pocket of her coat. "But it could be perfect for you and your little boy. You really do need to keep an open mind when you see it, though," she warned. "Don't judge it as is. Look for the possibilities.

"You'll be met at the address on the back." She held out a white, pearlescent business card. "The owner's representative will be there at ten tomorrow morning. A man by the name of Erik Sullivan. He's quite knowledgeable about the property, so feel free to ask him anything that will help you decide whether you want the place or not. You should keep an open mind about him, too.

"I have to run now. Double-parked," she said, explaining her rush but not the warning. "If you like what you see, I'll see you tomorrow afternoon."

Rory took the pretty little card. Neatly hand-printed on the back was an address outside Port Orchard, a short ferry ride across the sound from Seattle.

With questions piling up like leaves in the fall, she glanced back up.

The woman was gone.

Seeing no sign of her in the Pacific Northwest mist that was closer to fog than rain, she looked back to the shimmery little card.

The past fourteen months had left her without faith in much of anything anymore. The sudden, devastating loss of her husband to an uninsured drunk driver who'd run a red light. The whispered and crushing comments about their marriage that she'd overheard at his funeral. The exodus from her life of people she'd once thought of as family and friends. Each event had been shattering in its own right. Together, they'd made her afraid to trust much of anything. Or anyone.

And that had been before she'd lost the job Harvey Bleaker had said was hers for as long as she needed it.

The lovely woman with the bookish glasses had appeared out of nowhere. As if by magic, she'd disappeared into the mist the same way, like some sort of a fairy godmother dressed in faux fur and carrying Coach.

Dead certain her sleepless nights had just caught up with her, Rory dropped the card into the open compartment on the console. Whatever had just happened had to be either too good to be true or came with a spiderweb of strings attached to it.

Probably, undoubtedly, both.

Still, she, Tyler and the for-rent section of the newspaper were going apartment hunting in the morning. Having just picked up a check for the small down payment she'd put on the house she hadn't been able to buy, less fees, she had enough for three or four months' rent and expenses. In the meantime, feeling a desperate need for either magic or a miracle, she figured she had nothing to lose by checking out the address on that card.

She just hoped that this Erik Sullivan would be as accepting of her circumstances as Mrs. Cornelia Hunt seemed to be.

[faint offset text from facing page, illegible]

Chapter One

"Are we lost, Mom?"

"No, honey. We're not lost." Parked on the dirt shoulder of a narrow rural road, Rory frowned at the building a few dozen yards away. "I'm just not sure this is the right address."

"If we can't find it, can we go to the Christmas place?"

"We'll see, sweetie. We're looking for a new place to live right now."

"I don't want a new one."

"I know you don't," she murmured. Freckles dotted Tyler's nose. His sandy hair, neatly combed when they'd left the house, fell over his forehead, victim of the breeze that had blown in when she'd lowered his window to get a better look at the address on the roadside mailbox.

Nudging wisps back from his forehead, she smiled. "But we need one. And I need you to help me pick it out. It's our adventure, remember?"

"Then can we go to the Christmas place?"

They had seen a banner for a holiday festival in nearby Port Orchard when they'd driven off the ferry. Tyler had been asking about it ever since.

Everything she'd read last night on the internet made the area around the shoreline community a few miles around the bend sound nearly idyllic. The part of her that didn't want to get her hopes up knew that could simply have been good marketing by its chamber of commerce. The part that desperately needed this not to be a wild-goose chase focused on getting them moving.

"Not today, I'm afraid." She hated to say no, but housing had to be their first priority. "We don't have time."

It was nine fifty-five. They were to meet the seller's representative at ten o'clock.

Reminding Tyler of that, and agreeing that, yes, they were still "exploring," she pulled his hood over his head and glanced to the structure surrounded by a few winter-bare trees, dead grass and a wet patch of gravel that, apparently, served as a parking lot.

The address on the mailbox matched the one on the card. The structure, however, bore no resemblance at all to a residence. The two-story flat-roofed rectangle of a building faced a partial view of a little marina two city blocks away and backed up to a forest of pines.

A long, narrow sign above the porch read Harbor Market & Sporting Goods. Signs by the screened door read Fresh Espresso and Worms and Closed Until Spring.

Mailboxes farther up the road indicated homes tucked back in the trees. The only vehicle to be seen, however, was hers. With no sign of life in either direction, she was about to pull out her cell phone to check the address with Phil Granger when she remembered what the woman had said.

She'd warned her to keep an open mind when she saw the place. To look for possibilities.

The potential goose chase was also, apparently, a scavenger hunt.

A narrow driveway curved around the back of the building and disappeared down a slight hill. Thinking there might be a house or cottage beyond the gate blocking it, she grabbed the shoulder bag that held everything from animal crackers to a Zen meditation manual and gamely told her little boy they were going to look around while they waited for the person they were to meet to show up.

The damp breeze whipped around them, scattering leaves in their path as they left the car. With a glance toward the threatening sky, she was about to reconsider her plan when the relative quiet gave way to a squeak and the hard slam of a door.

Tyler froze.

Across twenty feet of gravel, she watched six feet two inches of broad-shouldered, purely rugged masculinity in a fisherman's sweater and worn jeans cross the store's porch and jog down its three steps.

"Sorry about that." His apology came quickly, his voice as deep as the undercurrents in the distant water. "I didn't mean to startle you. I keep forgetting to fix the spring."

The breeze blew a little harder, rearranging the otherwise neat cut of his slightly overlong dark hair. He didn't seem to notice the wind. Or the cold bite that came with it. All lean, athletic muscle, he strode toward them, his glance shifting between her and the child who'd smashed himself against her leg.

That glance turned questioning as he stopped six feet from where she'd rooted herself in the driveway.

"Are you Mrs. Linfield?"

Surprise colored the deep tones of his voice. Or maybe what she heard was disbelief. His pewter-gray eyes ran from the wedge of auburn hair skimming her shoulders, over the camel peacoat covering her black turtleneck and jeans and up from the toes of her low-heeled boots. His perusal was quick, little more than an impassive flick of his glance. Yet she had the unnerving feeling he'd imagined her every curve in the brief moments before she realized he was waiting for her to speak.

"I didn't think anyone was here." The admission came in a rush. "I didn't see a car, so we were just going to look around—"

"I flew over. Floatplane," he explained, hitching his head in the direction of the water. "It's down at the marina."

"I'm Erik Sullivan." Stepping closer, he extended his hand. His rugged features held strength, a hint of fearlessness. Or maybe it was boldness. Despite its lingering shadow, the square line of his jaw appeared recently shaved. He looked hard and handsome and when he smiled, faint though the expression was, he radiated a positively lethal combination of quiet command and casual ease. "I'm handling the sale of this property for my grandparents."

"You're a Realtor?"

"Actually, I build boats. I'm just taking care of this for them."

Her hand had disappeared in his.

She could feel calluses at the base of his fingers. He worked with his hands. Built boats with them, he'd said. What kind, she had no idea. The white-gold Rolex on his thick wrist seemed to indicate he was successful at it, though. The words *capable* and *accomplished* quickly flashed in her mind, only to succumb to less definable impressions as she became aware of the heat of his palm, the strength in his grip and the deliberate way he held that strength in check.

What she felt mostly, though, was a wholly unexpected sense of connection when her eyes met his.

Everything inside her seemed to go still.

She'd experienced that sensation only once before; the

first time Curt had taken her hand. It had been a fleeting thing, little more than an odd combination of awareness and ease that had come out of nowhere, but it had dictated the direction of her life from that moment on.

As if she'd just touched lightning, she jerked back, curling her fingers into her palm, and took a step away. The void left in her heart by the loss of her husband already felt huge. It seemed to widen further as she instinctively rejected the thought of any sort of connection to this man, imagined or otherwise. Because of what she'd learned since Curt's death, it was entirely possible that what she'd thought she'd had with her husband—the closeness, the love, the very rightness of the life they'd shared—hadn't existed at all.

Having struggled with that awful possibility for over a year, she wasn't about to trust what she'd felt now.

Conscious of the quick pinch of Erik's brow, totally embarrassed by her abrupt reaction, she rested her hand on her son's shoulder. Just as she would have introduced her little guy, the big man gave the child a cautious smile and motioned her toward the building.

"The main entrance to the living quarters is around back, but we can go through the market. Come on and I'll show you around."

Whatever he thought of her reaction to him, he seemed gentleman enough to ignore it.

She chose to ignore it, too.

Living quarters, he'd said?

"There isn't a separate house here?" she asked, urging Tyler forward as the sky started to leak.

"There's plenty of room to build if that's what a buyer wants to do. The parcel is a little over three acres. Living on premises has certain advantages, though." He checked the length of his strides, allowing them to keep up. "Shortens the commute."

If she smiled at that, Erik couldn't tell, not with the fall of cinnamon hair hiding her profile as she ushered the boy ahead of her.

Mrs. Rory Linfield wasn't at all what he had expected. But then, the new owner of the building next door to Merrick & Sullivan Yachting hadn't given him much to go on. He wasn't sure what the elegant and refined wife of Harry Hunt was doing with the building Harry had apparently given her as a wedding gift—other than providing Erik and his business partner an interesting diversion with her total renovation of its interior. It had been his offhand comment to Cornelia, though, about a place he'd be glad to sell if Harry was still into buying random pieces of property, that had led him to describe the property his grandparents had vacated nearly a year ago.

The conversation had prompted a call from Cornelia yesterday. That was when she'd told him she knew of a widow in immediate need of a home and a means to produce an income.

When she'd said *widow,* he'd immediately pictured someone far more mature. More his parents' age. Fifty-something. Sixty, maybe. With graying hair. Or at least a few wrinkles. The decidedly polished, manicured and attractive auburn-haired woman skeptically eyeing the sign for Fresh Espresso and Worms as she crossed the wood-planked porch didn't look at all like his idea of a widow, though. She looked more like pure temptation. Temptation with pale skin that fairly begged to be touched, a beautiful mouth glossed with something sheer pink and shiny, and who was easily a decade younger than his own thirty-nine years.

He hadn't expected the cute little kid at all.

He opened the door, held it for them to pass, caught her soft, unexpectedly provocative scent. Following them inside, he had to admit that, mostly, he hadn't anticipated

the sucker punch to his gut when he'd looked from her
very kissable mouth to the feminine caution in her big
brown eyes. Or the quick caution he'd felt himself when
she'd pulled back and her guarded smile had slipped into
place.

What he'd seen in those dark and lovely depths had
hinted heavily of response, confusion and denial.

A different sort of confusion clouded her expression
now.

He'd turned on the store's fluorescent overheads when
he'd first arrived. In those bright industrial lights, he
watched her look from the rows of bare, utilitarian grocery shelving to the empty dairy case near the checkout
counter and fix her focus on a kayak suspended from the
ceiling above a wall of flotation devices. Sporting goods
still filled the back shelves. After the original offer to buy
the place fully stocked had fallen through, he'd donated
the grocery items to a local food bank. That had been
months ago.

The little boy tugged her hand. "Why is the boat up
there, Mom?"

"For display. I think," she replied quietly, like someone
talking in a museum.

"How come?"

"So people will notice it." She pointed to a horizontal
rack on the back wall that held three more. Oars and water
skis stood in rows on either side. "It's easier to see than
those back there."

With his neck craned back, his little brow pinched.

"Are we gonna live in a store?"

"No, sweetie. We're just…" From the uncertainty in
her expression, it seemed she wasn't sure what they were
doing at the moment. "Looking," she concluded.

Her glance swung up. "You said this belongs to your
grandparents?"

"They retired to San Diego," he told her, wondering what her little boy was doing now as the child practically bent himself in half looking under a display case. There were no small children in his family. The yachting circles he worked and played in were strictly adult. Any exposure he had to little kids came with whatever family thing his business partner could talk him into attending with him. Since he managed to limit that to once every couple of years, he rarely gave kids any thought. Not anymore.

"They'd had this business for over fifty years," he explained, his attention already back on why the property was for sale. "It was time they retired."

The delicate arches of her eyebrows disappeared beneath her shiny bangs. "Fifty years?"

"Fifty-three, actually. They'd still be running the place if Gramps hadn't hurt his back changing one of the light fixtures." Erik had told him he'd change the tube himself. Just as he'd helped with other repairs they'd needed over the years. But the Irish in John Sullivan tended to make him a tad impatient at times. "He can be a little stubborn."

"Did he fall?"

"He just twisted wrong," he told her, conscious of the quick concern in her eyes, "but it took a couple of months for him to be able to lift anything. Grandma picked up as much slack as she could, but those two months made them decide it was time to tackle the other half of their bucket list while they could both still get around."

Her uncertainty about her surroundings had yet to ease. Despite her faint smile, that hesitation marked her every step as she moved farther in, checking out the plank-board floor, the single checkout counter, the old, yellowing acoustic tiles on the ceiling. Watching her, he couldn't help but wonder how she would do on a ladder, changing four-foot-long fluorescent tubes in a fixture fourteen feet off the floor. Or how she'd wrestle the heavy wood ladder up from the basement in the first place.

Since Cornelia had specifically asked if the business was one a woman could handle on her own, he'd also thought his prospective buyer would be a little sturdier.

Rather than indulge the temptation to reassess what he could of her frame, hidden as it was by her coat, anyway, he focused on just selling the place.

"The original building was single story," he told her, since the structure itself appeared to have her attention. "When they decided to add sporting goods, they incorporated the living area into the store, built on in back and added the upstairs.

"The business is seasonal," he continued when no questions were forthcoming. "Since summer and fall recreation provided most of their profit, they always opened in April and closed the first of October. That gave them the winter for vacations and time to work on their projects."

It was a good, solid business. One that had allowed his grandparents to support their family—his dad, his aunts. He told her that, too, because he figured that would be important to a woman who apparently needed to support a child on her own. What he didn't mention was that after the first sale fell through, the only other offers made had been too ridiculously low for his grandparents to even consider.

Because there were no other reasonable offers in sight, he wasn't about to let them pass up Cornelia's offer to buy it—if this particular woman was interested in owning it. He hadn't even balked at the terms of the sale that required his agreement to help get the business back up and running.

Selling the place would rid him of the obligation to keep it up. Even more important than ending the time drain of weekly trips from Seattle to make sure nothing was leaking, broken or keeping the place from showing well was that his grandparents had been the last of his relatives in this part of the sound. Once the place was sold, he had no reason to ever come back.

Considering all the plans he'd once had for his own life there, nearly all of which had failed rather spectacularly, that suited him just fine.

His potential project had yet to ask a single question. He, however, had a few of his own.

"Have you owned a business before?"

He thought the query perfectly reasonable.

She simply seemed to find it odd.

"Never," she replied, sounding as if she'd never considered running one, either. Still holding her little boy's hand, she set her sights on the open door behind the L-shaped checkout counter. "Is that the way to the living area?"

He told her it was, that it led into a foyer.

Wanting a whole lot more information than she'd just given, he followed her with the child looking back at him over the shoulder of his puffy blue jacket.

The instant he met the child's hazel eyes, the boy ducked his head and turned away.

With a mental shrug, Erik focused on the mom. She looked very much like the spa-and-Pilates type married to some of his high-end clients. Yet the car she drove was a total contrast—economical, practical. "Are you into outdoor sports?"

"We have bicycles," came her distracted reply.

"Mountain or street?"

"Street."

"For racing or touring?"

"Just for regular riding."

"Do you know anything about mountain bikes?"

"Is there a difference?"

That she'd had to ask had him moving on. "What about hiking or camping?"

"Not so much."

"Water sports? Do you windsurf, paddleboard, water ski?"

"Not really."

He took that as a no. "Do you know anything about sporting goods?"

Clearly on a mission of her own, she answered his last query with a puzzled glance and moved past the stairs, one set leading up, the other down, and into a spacious living room.

The empty downstairs space was interrupted only by the kitchen's long island near one end and anchored by a ceiling-high stone fireplace at the other. The bare walls all bore a pristine coat of latte-colored paint.

It was toward the kitchen that she motioned. "Mind if I look back there?"

Not at all pleased with her responses, he told her he didn't and watched her head for the glass-faced cupboards.

Her sandy-haired son darted straight to one of the large picture windows lining the opposite wall.

"Have you ever worked retail?" he asked her.

"Never," she replied once more.

"Wow, Mom. Look! It has a park!"

Rory's glance cut to where her little boy pressed his nose to the wide window near the fireplace. A large meadow stretched to a forest of pines. Between the dawning potential in the place and the feel of the tall, decidedly distracting male frowning at her back, she hadn't noticed the expansive and beautiful view until just then.

What she noticed now was her son's grin.

That guileless smile added another plus to her escalating but decidedly cautious interest in what surrounded her. "It sure does, sweetie. But stay with me. Okay?"

Yanking his unzipped jacket back over the shoulder of his Spider-Man sweatshirt, he hurried to her, his little voice dropping as he glanced to the man who remained on the other side of the white oak island.

"Does he live here?" he asked, pointing behind him.

She curled her hand over his fingers. "It's not polite to point," she murmured. "And no. He lives somewhere else."

"Where?"

"I don't know, honey."

"But it's a long way, huh?"

"Why do you say that?"

"'Cause he said he came in a plane. It floated here."

From the corner of her eye, she noticed the big man's brow lower in confusion.

"He came by *floatplane*," she clarified, easing confusion for them both. "It's a plane that can land on water. It flies just like any other."

"Oh." Tyler screwed up his nose, little wheels spinning. "Why didn't he make him a boat?"

He remembered what Erik had said he did for a living.

There wasn't much Tyler heard that he ever forgot. She'd come to regard the ability, however, as a double-edged sword. While her bright little boy absorbed information like an industrial-strength sponge, there were things she knew he'd overheard that she truly hoped he'd forgotten by now. Things certain relatives had said that had confused him at the time, hurt him and made her even more fiercely protective of him than she'd been even before he'd lost his dad.

Since no response came from the other side of the island, she told Tyler it was possible that Mr. Sullivan did have a boat, but that it was really none of their business. Right now, they needed to look at the rest of the house.

There were certain advantages to a five-year-old's short attention span. Already thrilled by the "park," Tyler promptly forgot his interest in the boat their guide did or did not have and, like her, poked his head into the pantry, the mudroom and downstairs closets.

There was no denying his attraction to the cubbyhole he found in one of the upstairs bedrooms. Her own interest, however, she held in check. A person couldn't be disappointed if she didn't get her expectations up to begin with.

The property was nothing she would have considered even a week ago. It had none of the little neighborhood atmosphere she'd looked for. None of the coziness she'd craved for herself and her son. It felt too remote. Too foreign. Too…unexpected.

Her option was an unknown apartment in an as yet undetermined area near a job she still had to find.

Her hopes rose anyway, her mind racing as Erik led her back down from the three bedrooms and two baths that would be more than adequate for her and her son.

Phil had said to keep an open mind about this place.

Despite its drawbacks, it was, indeed, full of possibilities. But it wasn't just Tyler's surprisingly positive reactions or the idyllic views from some of the windows that tempered her misgivings. What Phil hadn't mentioned was that this wouldn't just be a place to live. It would be her source of income.

She could have her own business. Be her own boss. That meant the means to support her son would be dependent on her, not on someone else with obligations or agendas of their own. It would be up to her if she succeeded or failed. And while the thought brought as much anxiety as anticipation, mostly it brought a surprising hint of reprieve.

She could start over here. She could finally, truly move on.

By the time they'd worked their way back downstairs, Tyler knew which room he wanted to be his. He wasn't quite so sure what to make of their tour guide, though. Every time he'd looked over his shoulder to see if Erik was still with them, he'd moved closer to her or tightened his grip on her hand.

Considering the man's easy self-assurance, it struck her as odd that he appeared equally undecided about Tyler. Because he'd yet to say a word to her son, she wasn't sure if he simply didn't know how to relate to small children or if he was one of those people, like her father-in-law, who felt a child was to be seen and not heard and otherwise ignored until they became of an age to engage in meaningful conversation.

Maternal instincts on alert, the moment they reached the foyer, she asked Tyler to see if he could spot deer in the woods from the living room window. He was barely out of earshot when she felt Erik Sullivan's disconcerting presence beside her.

"Your son seems to like the place," he pointed out, joining her by the mahogany newel post. "What about you? You haven't said much."

Erik would admit to not being particularly adept at deciphering women, even when they did speak. *No* often meant *yes. Don't* often mean *go ahead. Nothing* always meant *something,* though finding out what that something was could be akin to pulling an anchor out of dried cement. But this woman hadn't given him so much as a hint about any conclusion she might have drawn.

"Do you have any questions?" he prompted.

"When did you say the store usually opened for business?"

"April. The first or second week."

She lifted her chin, her thoughts apparently coming in no particular order.

"Phil Granger said you know I can't qualify for a mortgage just now."

"We're aware of that," he assured her.

"Were your grandparents planning to carry the mortgage themselves?"

"A second party will carry it. So," he prodded, "you're interested, then?"

She wanted to smile. He could see the expression trying to light the flecks of bronze in her deep brown eyes. She just wouldn't let it surface.

"That depends on what they want for it. And the terms. How much are they asking?"

He should have been relieved by her interest. Would have been had she been even remotely qualified to take on the store.

"That's...negotiable."

"But they must have a price in mind."

"Do you have *any* business experience?"

It was as clear to Rory as the doubt carved in his handsome face that he had serious concerns about her ability to make a go of the store his grandparents were selling. Unflattering as his obvious skepticism was, she couldn't fault him for it. They had run the business for decades. They'd probably poured their hearts and souls into the place that had defined them for years. This man hadn't had to tell her for her to know how much the store and their home had meant to them. The shelving in the spare room upstairs—his grandma's sewing room, he'd said—had been built by his dad. The beautiful, lacquered banister beside them had been lathed by his grandfather.

He'd casually mentioned those things in passing. With his big hand splayed over the grapefruit-size mahogany ball atop the newel post, his thumb absently rubbing its shiny finish, she realized this place mattered to him, too.

Her only concern now was that he trust her with it.

She took a step closer, lowering her voice so Tyler couldn't overhear.

"It's not that I've never had a job," she informed him

quietly. "I was a file clerk while I worked on an associate's degree. After that, I spent four years as a legal secretary before Tyler came along. I went back to work transcribing documents at another law firm ten months ago. I'd still be doing that if they hadn't let me go because the firm merged and they cut my job."

Skipping over the five-year gap in her résumé, she aimed for the heart of his concern. "I've just never owned a business. Or sold anything other than whatever the PTA was selling to raise money for school projects.

"I'll admit that when I got here," she hurried on, hoping he'd overlook that last part, "the last thing I expected was a store. But you said it's a good, solid business. If your grandparents didn't usually open it until April, that would give me four months to figure out what needs to be done and how to do it." All she had to do was get past the daunting little fact that she had no idea where to start.

"Look," she murmured, too tired after too many sleepless nights to care how much of herself she exposed. "I'll admit I don't know a…a…"

"A bivy sack from a bobber?" he suggested.

"Exactly. And until now," she said, muscling on, "I'd honestly never thought about owning anything like this. The only sports I know anything about are tennis and golf." And that was only because her husband had wanted her to fit in at the club. She was so not the rugged, outdoors type. "But I'll do whatever I have to do to provide for my son.

"This could be a good place to raise him. He could help me in the store. I think he'd love that. He'd even have his own park," she pointed out, thinking of how badly she wanted them gone from the exclusive community that had come to feel like a prison. She'd hoped for a normal neighborhood, but breathing room would be a good thing, too.

"I'll never be able to replace the security he had before his dad died, but it's up to me to give him as much stability as I can." Her voice fell with her final admission. "I think I can do that here."

Her last words were as soft as the utter conviction in her eyes. Erik saw a plea there, too. Quiet. A little raw. And a lot uncomfortable for him to witness in the moments before he glanced to where her son seemed to be counting something at the window.

He'd been about that age—five or so, if he had to guess—when his grandfather had put him to work stacking canned goods on shelves. After that, he'd practically begged to come over so he could help.

He'd once thought this would be a good place to raise a child, too.

"There's one other thing," she admitted, her voice still quiet. "Tyler has never lived anywhere other than in the house we're leaving. We have to be out in three days. Until the job thing happened, I'd thought we'd be settled in our new house well before Christmas. He didn't have a very good one last year and it would be really nice to find a place that I don't have to move him from again." Practicality, or maybe it was weariness, kept her tone utterly matter-of-fact. "So how much is it?" she asked. "And how do I make this happen?"

He didn't know which struck him more just then: her absolute determination to do whatever she had to do to care for her child or the naked vulnerability lurking in the depths of her eyes.

As if she knew what he saw, her glance hit the floor.

Her determination to hide that vulnerability pulled at something unfamiliar deep in his chest, even as he steeled himself against it.

He hadn't been told how she'd been widowed. Or how long she and her child had been on their own. He had no idea if her marriage had been as good as his parents', as much a failure as his own had been or some form of tolerable in-between. He knew only from what she'd said about her child's loss that it was entirely possible she still grieved the man she'd lost, too.

He wasn't a particularly sensitive or sympathetic man. Or so he'd been informed by his ex-wife and certain of the arm candy who trolled the circles he moved in. But he wasn't at all comfortable being privy to something so personal. It disturbed him even more to find himself wondering what it would be like to mean that much to a woman.

Equally unsettling was the fact that an hour ago, she hadn't even known the store existed. "I can't give you the terms."

She hadn't a clue what she was getting into.

He knew for a fact that he was no longer comfortable with what he'd agreed to do himself.

"My agreement with Cornelia...Mrs. Hunt," he corrected, "is that she or her assistant will discuss those details with you."

Reaching into the back pocket of his jeans, he extracted one of the same pearlescent cards Phil had given her yesterday. "Did you take the ferry or do the loop through Tacoma?"

"Ferry."

"Which one?"

"Southworth. It lands at Fauntleroy."

By land or water, either way it would take her a while to get back to Seattle.

"Then I'll give you directions to their office from the dock. I have another meeting in Seattle at noon." Card in hand, he pulled his cell phone from another pocket and keyed in a number.

With the instrument to his ear, he turned away, started to pace.

Rory glanced at her watch. It was already after eleven o'clock.

She was about to mention that when she remembered his mode of transport was infinitely faster than hers. He was already into his conversation with Phil, anyway. She couldn't hear what he said, though. She knew only that he looked oddly resigned when he turned a minute later to inform her that Phil wanted to talk to her.

By the time the woman who had appeared out of nowhere yesterday told her everything was ready to proceed with the sale and confirmed their meeting that afternoon, Rory couldn't shake the feeling that nothing could possibly be as simple as Phil had made it sound—and that Erik Sullivan had more of a role in the sale than anyone was letting on.

Chapter Two

The directions Rory had been given led her to the Ballard neighborhood in northwestern Seattle and a weathered, two-story redbrick building much like the others along an old business section of the waterfront. What distinguished the structure was the trail of plaster dust and debris leading from the open front door to the Wolf Construction Dumpster at the curb.

Inside, sheets of milky construction plastic masked two stories of interior scaffolding and what appeared to be something grand under construction. The filmy barriers did little to deaden the occasional clatter and boom of interior demolition. The noise was muffled considerably, however, behind the closed door of the only completed space—an unexpectedly feminine and elegant ground floor corner conference room in shades of ivory and pale taupe with a view of a marina, Shilsole Bay and snow-capped Hurricane Ridge beyond.

The long banks of ivory-draped windows caught Tyler's

attention the moment they'd walked in. Rory had thought the boats in the inlet had drawn him. Until she noticed Erik.

A walkway ran behind the buildings. She could see him outside, pacing past the rows of windows, bare-masted sailboats bobbing in the background. Apparently oblivious to the chill, he had one hand in a front pocket of his jeans, his head down against the breeze as he talked on his cell phone.

He did not look happy.

Logic told her he could be talking about anything. But the unease joining her curiosity and uncertainty over this meeting made her fairly certain his scowl had something to do with her.

"We're so glad you liked the place," said Phil, leading her across the floor, the click of her heels on polished oak suddenly hushed by the pale blue Aubusson rug. "With everything so unsettled for you, we didn't know if you'd see the advantages of taking on a business right now. Especially one that you might not ordinarily have considered."

Wearing a cream blouse and slacks slung with a thin gold belt, the woman Rory met yesterday took her and Tyler's coats and motioned to one of the Queen Anne chairs at the circular conference table. The light from the ornate crystal chandelier above it made the mahogany surface gleam like glass. "Cornelia did feel you'd consider it, though," she added, "given your circumstances."

"Which are very close to what mine were at one time," came a voice from a small alcove.

A statuesque, elegantly mature lady in pale lavender cashmere emerged from the washroom, carrying roses she'd just freshened. Her silver-blond hair was coiled in a chic chignon at her nape. Diamonds glinted from her ears. The rock on her left hand, a huge pink diamond surrounded by a dozen of brilliant white, flashed in its platinum setting as she set the vase on a marble credenza with a quiet clink.

"Please pardon the mess out there, Rory. We're a work in progress at the moment. I'm Cornelia Hunt," she said, intent on putting her guest at ease as she held out her hand. "It's a pleasure to finally meet you."

Feeling a distinct connection to Alice after she'd slipped down the rabbit hole, Rory clasped the woman's hand. She had dressed that morning in a casual black turtleneck and skinny denims to look at properties and apartments, not to meet well-dressed ladies in what could have passed for a drawing room in a palace.

"The pleasure's mine," she returned, fighting the urge to curtsy.

"You only met briefly, so I'll officially introduce you to Felicity Granger. Phil is my assistant. She's also an academic counselor at the university. She's really rather brilliant at helping others with their life decisions, so I brought her in to help me with my work." Her green eyes seemed to twinkle as she smiled. "What have you been told about the arrangements so far?"

"Hardly anything. The man who showed us around… Erik," she identified, still aware of him pacing, "wouldn't even give me the price."

"I don't doubt that you have questions," Cornelia conceded. "I'll have Phil start answering yours and explain the details while I get us some coffee. Or would you prefer tea?"

Rory told her coffee was fine, thank you. And that yes, cocoa for Tyler would be nice. Even as she spoke, she wasn't at all sure what struck her as more incongruous just then: that Cornelia Fairchild Hunt, the very pleasant wife of a reportedly eccentric computer-genius billionaire, was getting her coffee. Or the mound of dingy canvas mail sacks piled beside a delicate French provincial writing desk.

On the desk's surface, dozens of what appeared to be opened letters teetered in stacks.

Phil took the chair next to Rory. Seeing what had her attention, she adjusted her overlarge glasses and leaned toward her.

"There was an article in the Seattle *Washtub* recently about how Cornelia helped a young entrepreneur get the break she needed with her business. Ever since then, requests have poured in by email and snail mail for her in care of the newspaper and the offices of HuntCom asking for her help from other young women. And for them. Like you," she explained. "The reporter who wrote the article said she's bringing another sackful over this afternoon."

"A reporter is part of this?"

"Don't worry," Phil hastily assured. "Cornelia wants to stay under the radar with her project and she trusts Shea Weatherby to help her with that. As for anyone else we might need to talk with, we only identify our clients to those directly involved in her situation."

The assertion was hugely reassuring to Rory. She'd already supplied enough fodder for gossip in certain social circles to last a lifetime. Nearly every member of those circles would have sold their summer homes to mingle with a Hunt, too. But all that mattered to her just then was that this meeting was confidential. Her relationship with her in-laws was strained enough without word getting out and embarrassing them because their son's widow apparently needed to be bailed out by strangers. For Tyler's sake, she needed to make as few waves with them as possible.

Thinking about her in-laws reminded her that she needed to call them about Christmas.

"The volume of requests Cornelia is receiving," Phil continued, mercifully sidetracking her from the stomach-knotting thought, "is why she needed to hire help. I just love what she's doing."

"I really am at a loss here," Rory admitted. "What *is* she doing?"

"She's being what the first woman she helped called her," her assistant replied. "A fairy godmother."

She had a fairy godmother?

"On to the details." Phil pushed a pale blue folder toward her, the snowflake polish on her nails glittering. "If these terms are agreeable to you, Cornelia will purchase the property you saw from the owners and you will purchase it from her for the amount stated on line one. To keep everything legal and as simple as possible, your down payment will be one dollar. Your balance will be interest-free with the first payment due September first. You'll have had five months of cash flow by then."

Disbelief held Rory's tone to nearly a whisper. The number couldn't possibly be right. "The property has to be worth three times this."

"Oh, it is. And that's what Cornelia will pay the owners for it. But that's your price. Of course, there is more to the sale."

Ah, yes, Rory thought, unable to understand why Cornelia would take such a loss for her. The strings.

"Cornelia has added a few perks," Phil chose to call them. "She believes the best route to success is to have a good adviser. Since it's understandable that you'd know little about this particular business and since the Sullivan's grandson is reasonably acquainted with it, she arranged for Erik to be your mentor for the next six months. He'll help you with your inventory, suppliers, getting part-time help and whatever else it will take to get your new venture up and running.

"The two of you can determine how often you need to meet, but there will be a status meeting here once a month.

Of course, I'm available to both of you together or individually at any time. At the end of the six months, if you're on track with your business plan, Erik will have fulfilled his mentor agreement, and you'll be on your own. All we ask," she concluded, as if she'd rather expected the stunned silence coming from beside her, "is for your discretion in discussing the work we do here."

Phil sat back, smiling.

Rory couldn't seem to move.

Poof. Just like that. The property her little boy had fallen in love with that morning—and the business that came with it—could be hers.

The reality of it didn't want to sink in. Yet even in her disbelief what registered most was that her new life included a man who she strongly suspected didn't want to work with her at all.

"This Erik," she said, caution competing with amazement as Cornelia joined them with a tray of tall porcelain mugs. "May I ask the terms of his agreement with you?"

Taking the chair on the opposite side of her, Cornelia passed mugs to her and Phil. "It's nothing complicated. I just requested that he help you with the business if I buy the property for the Sullivans' asking price."

"But why did he agree to that?"

"Because he wants a decent price for his grandparents and I offered him one. He's been taking care of the property for them, so I also imagine he'd like to be free of that responsibility. I don't think he begrudges his grandparents his time. He sounds quite fond of them," she offered, approval in the soft lines of her face. "But he's a busy man."

Rory remembered his strong, workingman's hands, the calluses she'd felt brush her palm. Right behind the thought came the disquieting memory of what his touch had elicited. "He said he builds boats."

"Oh, they're more than boats. He and his business partner build world-class sailing sloops. Their boatworks is down past the marina, but their sales and rental office is next door. J.T., one of my stepsons," she said, identifying Harry's second oldest, "commissioned one from him years back. He said Erik is the only man he'd ever do business with on a handshake. If you knew my stepson, you'd know that respect for someone's character doesn't get any greater than that."

Her carefully penciled eyebrows arched as she offered cream and sugar. "Did you find him disagreeable?"

Disturbing, yes. Disagreeable? She couldn't honestly say they'd disagreed about anything. "No."

"Are you not wanting help?"

Rory shook her head. She'd be a fool to turn it down. "I'm sure he has far more information about how the market is run than anything I can even begin to find on my own."

The unguarded admission brought Cornelia's smile back. "Then it's a win-win for everyone."

Baffled by the woman, more uncertain than she wanted to admit about her mentor, Rory touched the handle of her mug. "Please don't think I'm not beyond grateful, Mrs. Hunt—"

"It's Cornelia," the woman said graciously.

"Cornelia," Rory corrected. "But I'm having a hard time making sense of all this. I understand from Phil that you helped someone else when she needed it. But why do you want to help *me* like this?"

"Because I can," she said simply. "My Harry gave me a ridiculously large amount of money for a wedding gift. Since I have the means, I decided to make it my mission to offer deserving young women a hand up when the going gets rough for them, or when they just need the right break.

"In your case," she admitted, "I know all too well what it's like to be financially strapped and the only parent. My first husband was a dear, but he left me in a real financial bind when he died. I had to sell my home, just as you've had to do. And I had to work hard to raise my girls."

She gave Rory's hand a pat, drew back her own. "From what we learned about you from your real estate agent—and other resources," she admitted, making it clear she thoroughly vetted the recipients of her largesse, "I don't doubt that you'll do what you must to make it work. Erik has proven himself to be an excellent businessman," she assured, as the opening door let in the back-up beep of a truck. "I'm sure you can trust him to help you succeed.

"Can't she, Erik?" she asked the man himself as he walked in.

Seeming oblivious to the way his presence suddenly filled the space, much less to the faint tension leaking from him in waves, Cornelia raised an eyebrow in his direction.

"Can't she what?" he replied.

"Trust your business judgment."

"It hasn't let me down so far."

The disarming smile he gave Cornelia and Phil seemed to come easily. The wattage, however, lowered considerably when it settled on her. Having met her eyes long enough to make her heart jerk, Rory watched him lower his glance to the older woman's coffee.

"Mind if I get some of that?"

"Not at all. The pot is fresh."

His heavy footsteps muffled by the carpet, Erik headed for the coffeemaker in the alcove. Behind him he could hear the elegant matron and the bookish blonde he'd met last week explaining that the paperwork for Rory's mortgage would be handled at a title company Monday afternoon. Since he had power of attorney for the sale for his grandparents, he and Cornelia had already agreed to take care of their business there that morning.

The Hunt name tended to eliminate delays.

He could hear the low, soft tones of Rory's responses, but he had no idea what she said. He was too busy telling himself that the next six months wouldn't be as bad as he'd feared.

They'd probably be worse.

He didn't question the sincerity of the rather shell-shocked-looking young woman reading the papers in front of her. Her determination to do what she had to do for her child had been nearly tangible to him. But her impulsiveness had raised about a dozen red flags.

Women spent more time making up their mind about buying a pair of shoes than she had about taking on something that would require a nearly 24/7 commitment. Especially at first. He knew. He ate, slept and breathed his own business. And that business was something he'd wanted since he was a kid. She'd only wanted the store since she'd learned about it that morning. She'd even admitted to knowing nothing about what she'd agreed to get herself into—which meant she'd take far more time than he'd planned on devoting to the care and feeding of her education.

It was that last part that he'd explained to his business partner when he'd called a while ago to tell him he'd still be tied up for a while. Pax had said not to worry about what he'd committed himself to. He'd cover for him if he needed time during the day to work with the store's new owner.

Though they'd never talked about the reasons for it, Pax knew how badly Erik wanted to be out from under that property. And why. They'd grown up together. Pax had been his best man. He'd also gone through the ugliness of his divorce with him by letting him take on however many projects it took to keep him too exhausted to think about anything else.

It had been seven years since the demise of his eight-year marriage, and Erik had long since recovered from what he had no intention of ever repeating again, but he already felt guilt about the time he'd be taking away from work. Especially with an April delivery date on their present work under construction, another client waiting for his final blueprints and two others hovering in the wings to get on their list.

Then there were their evening commitments with past and future clients. The holiday party season had just started—and Merrick & Sullivan Yachting never missed a business or philanthropic commitment.

With the women still talking, and feeling the tension creep up his back, he took his filled mug to the nearest window and rubbed at his neck. He'd do what he had to do where the woman behind him was concerned, and hope she wasn't the sort who required a lot of hand-holding to come up to speed. Heaven knew he wasn't a coddling sort of guy.

Erik took a sip of the coffee that was infinitely better than the sludge he and his partner had been brewing since their secretary had gone on maternity leave. It didn't help the situation that Mrs. Rory Linfield had a son. He'd made it a point over the past several years to avoid women with children. They tended to want more of a commitment than he was interested in. But that deliberate lack of exposure left him feeling less than capable when it came to anyone under four feet tall.

With his pretty little project deep in conversation, he looked out over the blue-tarped sailboats yawing in their slips. He and Pax had pulled their rental fleet out of the water last month, but farther up the shoreline, he could see the point that anchored the rest of their operation: the boatyard where they stored their boats over winter and the boatworks where they built their custom sailing yachts, one sloop at a time.

"How come that boat has a Santa on it?"

The little boy had walked over from two windows

down. Now, with his chin barely clearing the window-sill, the sandy-haired child pointed to a row of decorated sloops in the marina. Several had colored lights anchored fore and aft from the mainsail mast. One had a blow-up Santa at the helm.

Erik gave a shrug. "Some people just like to decorate their boats this time of year."

"How come?"

"Because they entertain on them," he said, thinking of the cocktail parties he and his partner had hosted on their respective sloops for their clients over the years. They had one scheduled next week. "Or maybe they're going to be in one of the boat parades." The floating parades were legend around the sound during the holidays.

The little boy's brow furrowed. Digesting what he'd been told, he said nothing else. For about five seconds, anyway.

"Do you have a boat?"

"I do."

"Do you decorate it?"

"I have."

"Do you put a Santa on it?"

"No."

"Oh," the child said.

He took another sip of coffee, waited for another question. When none was forthcoming, Erik tried to focus on the conversation behind him.

The small voice immediately cut in.

"I'm glad your house has a fireplace. So Santa can come down," Tyler explained, still looking out the window. "Mom said he can visit without one, but it's easier when he has a chimney."

It took a moment for the boy's conversational leap to make sense. Apparently since Santa was on his mind, any context was fair game.

"I've heard that about chimneys, too," he assured him. "And the house you saw isn't mine. It's my grandparents'."

The distinction apparently didn't matter.

"We have a fireplace in our house. But we didn't have a tree last time for him to put presents under." The small voice sounded utterly matter-of-fact. "Mom said this year won't be sad. We get a tree no matter what."

His mom had mentioned that he hadn't had a very good Christmas last year. Sad, the child had just called it. Yet Erik didn't let himself consider why that had been. Telling himself that her personal business was none of his, he murmured a distracted, "That's good," to her son and focused on the only business of hers he needed to be interested in. The store.

Cornelia had asked for his presence in case Rory had questions for him. He figured now was as good a time as any to see what those concerns might be.

The three females at the table glanced up as he approached.

It was Rory's dark eyes that he met.

"Is there anything you want to ask me about the property?"

Her shell-shocked look had yet to fade. With her ringless hand at the base of her throat, she slowly shook her head. "I don't even know where to start right now."

"Make a list as things occur to you," he told her. "I'll come by the market next week and we can go over it.

"The sale is being expedited," he told her, knowing now that part of the appeal of his grandparents' home, for her son, anyway, had been the fireplace his own family had gathered around at Christmas. "You can move in whenever you're ready. I'll check my schedule and Phil can set us up with a day and time next week to go over inventory."

He set his coffee on the table with a decisive clink and pulled his business card from his pocket. Walking around the table to give it to her, he watched her rise. As she did, his glance slid over what her coat had hidden earlier. The long black turtleneck she wore skimmed her feminine curves, molded the sweet shape of her hips.

She had the body of a dancer. Long, lithe and sexy as hell.

Masking his misgivings about having to deal with her, feeling them mount by the minute, he ignored the vague tightening in his gut. "Do you need help moving in?"

"No. I'm… No," Rory repeated, hating how flustered she felt. "But thank you." The last thing she wanted was to impose on this man. Considering what he'd been asked to do for her, she'd be obligated enough to him as it was. "I'd planned to be out Monday, so I've already arranged for movers."

She pushed back her bangs, revealing the pinch of her brow. "You really don't mind if I take things over before the sale closes?"

"You said you want to be settled before Christmas." He assumed now that that desire had something to do with putting up a tree. "The earlier you start, the sooner you can be."

Rory swallowed. Hard.

"Thank you."

He held out his card. "My office and cell numbers are on here. Call me if something comes up. I'll leave a key under the rock by the back porch. You'll get a full set at closing." His fingers brushed hers. Her skin felt cool to him, soft, and though he was trying not to notice anything in particular about her, he could have sworn he felt her trembling.

Without looking up, she palmed his card and clasped both hands in front of her.

"You're sure you're covered on the move?" he asked

"I'm positive. I arranged everything a couple of weeks ago."

Standing as close as he was, he caught the tremor in her

breath as she eased it out. He didn't doubt she felt overwhelmed with all that was happening for her. Yet she managed to maintain the composure that had her graciously assuring Cornelia that she truly needed nothing else as far as help was concerned. Something about that composure seemed practiced to him, though. It was as if she'd found herself in overwhelming or uncertain situations before and wasn't about to let anyone see how unsettled she really was.

She wouldn't look at him again. She seemed to know what he'd seen, and felt totally embarrassed being so exposed. A huge burden was being lifted from her slender shoulders, but she wasn't letting herself feel the relief of that weight. It appeared that admitting the scope of that relief would be admitting how truly desperate she'd begun to feel. So she just kept it all in, as if that was what she'd become accustomed to doing anyway, and turned to the women.

With a choked little laugh, she said she had no idea how to thank them.

Leaving her to figure it out, he looked to the matriarch running the show, thanked her for the coffee and headed for more familiar territory.

He'd given his word that he'd help. And he would. He never promised anything he didn't intend to deliver. But when he showed up for the meeting Phil arranged for him with Rory the following Wednesday, he discovered something about his charge that he hadn't anticipated.

The young widow with the sweet, sharp little boy might have looked as fragile as sea foam, but she had a stubborn streak as wide as Puget Sound.

Chapter Three

Erik hesitated at the store's front door. For years he'd simply walked in when the business had been open. After his grandparents had moved, he'd let himself in with his key. Since the sale had closed two days ago, he no longer had the right to come and go as he pleased from a place that had been part of his life for as long as he could remember.

The odd sense of having been displaced lingered as he rapped his knuckles on the frame of the screen door, and promptly disappeared the instant the inside door swung open. Even with her pretty features schooled into a smile of greeting, the unease in Rory's guarded expression made him suspect she was already having second thoughts about what she'd taken on.

Or so he was thinking when she let him in and his glance cut from the black hoodie and yoga pants molding her curves to the furniture behind her.

It looked as if every possession she owned sat piled in the interior of the market. Bedroom sets, tables, chairs, boxes.

"You said you didn't need any help moving in."

Good morning to you, too, Rory thought. "I didn't think I did," she said, stepping back for him to pass.

Deliberately overlooking the accusation shadowing his rugged features, she crossed her arms over her hoodie and the teal turtleneck and thermal undershirt layered beneath it. She wanted to believe her shiver had more to do with the chill in the large space than with the big man in the waffle-weave pullover and charcoal cargo pants. After all, the thermometer by the dairy case did read forty-nine degrees.

The man should wear a coat, she insisted to herself. It was easily ten degrees colder outside.

She turned on her heel to lead him inside where it was warmer. "The college kids I hired were only available long enough to drive the U-Haul over and unload it into the market," she explained, heading between the packing boxes that formed an aisle to the interior door. "It wasn't until we got here that they told me they wouldn't have time to carry everything to the rooms. They did take one of the beds upstairs, though." The thud of heavy hiking boots echoed behind her. In running shoes, her footsteps barely made a squeak. "A mattress, anyway," she qualified. "And a box of bedding." That had been huge.

Spending the past couple of nights on a hard floor would have guaranteed even less sleep than she usually managed. Even with a reasonably comfortable place to rest, she'd spent most of both nights trying not to disturb Tyler and listening to the building's unfamiliar creaks and groans while hoping to heaven she could make this store work.

"They'll come back to finish sometime next week," she continued, "so I've been taking in what I can by myself. Tyler's helping." Boxes too heavy to carry she'd emptied one armload at a time. The method wasn't the most efficient, but she now had one bathroom in order and the kitchen organized, except for the table and chairs. The old refectory table weighed a ton. She knew—she'd tried to move it last night.

She chafed her arms along her sleeves, winced a little when she rubbed a spot above the elbow that now sported the bruise she'd earned in the attempt. She had a matching one on the back of her shoulder. No longer hearing Erik's footfalls, she glanced around to see that he had stopped.

Across ten feet of worn plank flooring, she saw his dark eyebrows merge. "Isn't the furnace working?"

"It's working just fine."

"Then why is it so cold in here?"

"Because I'm not heating this big space until I have to. Fuel's expensive. By the way," she added, gratitude slipping into her voice, "thank you for having the tank filled. You saved me from running out of oil." She'd always had electric heat before. Not accustomed to an oil furnace, she hadn't realized the need for fuel until the man who'd performed the building inspection Sunday had showed her the tank and pointed out the gauge.

"The driver of the truck wouldn't leave an invoice," she told him. "So if you'll tell me what I owe you, I'll give you a check."

"You don't owe me anything."

"Yes, I do."

"No," he insisted, "you don't. Just think of it as a move-in present."

He obviously considered the matter settled. There seemed no doubt of that as he turned away to ponder the height and breadth of the obstacles blocking his view of the back of the store.

As appreciative as she was for his thoughtfulness, she couldn't accept his gift.

"Look." Hugging her arms a little tighter, she stepped in front of him. "I'm already not sure how I'll repay you for helping me get to know the store. I know you agreed to do it to help your grandparents sell this place," she conceded, which meant his benevolence definitely wasn't personal, "but I'd rather not be any more obligated to you than I already am. Or will be," she qualified, because other than make her acutely aware of his reluctant and very male presence, he hadn't done anything yet. "Okay?"

For a moment, he said nothing. He just let his deceptively easy glance slip over the quiet determination in her eyes before he headed to the checkout counter.

"Then don't accept it as a gift. Accept it because I'd rather work out here with heat."

Confusion preempted further defense. "I thought we were going to go over the inventory."

"That's the plan."

He carried a briefcase. A rather hefty one of scarred butterscotch leather and straps with buckles that had far more character than the sleek, unscuffed ones carried by other men she knew. As he set it on the scratched counter, she could see his burnished initials, worn shiny in places, above the equally worn lock. A section of stitching on the side looked new, as if it had recently been repaired. The case was old, she thought. It had history. And part of that history seemed to say that he'd rather keep and care for what he had than replace it.

Not appreciating how he'd dismissed her attempt to establish an understanding, she didn't bother to wonder why she found that so appealing.

"I thought we'd work where it's already warm. Inside," she pointed out, ever so reasonably. "We can sit at the island and go over the books in there."

"I meant the physical inventory. The stuff that's on the shelves and in the bins back there." He hitched his thumb over his shoulder. "I have a printout of what came with the sale, but those items have been sitting around for a year. You'll want to discount some of what you have and replace it with new merchandise. Things like sinkers, bobbers and leaders are fine, but creels and some of the stock that isn't packaged looks shopworn."

Rory hadn't a clue what he was talking about.

"Fishing gear," he explained, apparently sensing that.

Undaunted, she picked up a couple of the boxes from the cracked surface. She'd already decided the old laminate needed to go. "Then we'll work here at the counter."

The boxes had been emptied, Erik realized when she easily lifted two marked *Dishes* from where his grandfather had once kept displays of bug repellent and sunglasses. She removed two more, adding them to the only space available without blocking either doorway: the tops of three tall stacks of red-and-green bins marked *Christmas*.

She had to stretch to get them there. Jerking his glance from the enticing curve of her backside, he reached past her.

"Let me get that."

"Already have it," she insisted, and having placed the boxes, turned right into him.

Rock had more give to it.

The thought occurred vaguely as she bumped into his chest. Promptly bouncing back, she gasped a breath when his quick grip tightened on her upper arms. Her heart had barely slammed against her ribs when he pulled her forward to keep her from hitting the bins behind her and bringing the empty boxes down on their heads.

The freshness of soap and sea air clung to him. With her pulse scrambling, his grip tight on her bruise, she had no idea why the scents even registered. Her hand shot up, covering the back of his where it curved over the tender spot on her arm.

The pressure of his fingers eased.

With their bodies inches apart, she went as still as stone. Or maybe he froze first. She just knew that one moment she'd been intent on doing whatever she needed to do to make it clear that she wouldn't waste his time, and the next, the tension in his body and the warmth of his hands had seeped through to her skin, making her conscious of little more than…him.

Erik's eyes narrowed on hers an instant before she ducked her head. Slacking his grip, he dropped his hands. There'd been no mistaking the way she'd winced when he'd grabbed her.

Without thinking, he reached toward her again, touched the back of her hand where it now covered where his had been.

He hadn't thought he'd grabbed her that hard.

"Are you okay?"

At the concern in his voice, the caution in his touch, her head came back up. "I'm fine." Wanting to convince them both, she smiled. "Really."

His brow pinched as he drew his hand away once more.

Rory's breath slithered out. That small contact had been far too brief to elicit the loss she felt when he stepped back. Yet that sense of loss existed, sinking deeper into her chest with every heartbeat—unexpected, unwanted and feeling far too threatening under his quiet scrutiny.

A certain numbness had protected her since she'd lost what had felt like the other half of herself. Yet, as with the first time this man had touched her, something about him scraped at the edges of that barrier, made her conscious of things she truly didn't want to consider.

Out of nowhere, the need to be held sprang to mind. It was such a simple thing, so basic that she'd never truly considered it until it had been found and suddenly lost— that need for security, comfort, a sense of oneness. But she knew how rare it was to find that sense of belonging, and the need didn't feel simple at all. Not when she realized she was actually wondering what it would feel like to be folded against Erik's broad, undeniably solid chest. A woman would feel sheltered there. Safe from what troubled her. And for a few moments, anyway, free of the need to stand alone.

Shaken by her thoughts, by him, she started to move back, as much from the need behind the unexpected admissions as from the man who'd prompted them. The stacks behind her allowed her no escape at all.

His scrutiny narrowed. "If you're okay, why are you still holding your arm?"

She was holding in his touch. Realizing that, hoping he didn't, she promptly dropped her hand.

"It's nothing." Rattled, trying not to be, she shrugged. "It's just a little sore."

"Why?"

"Because I landed against the corner of a dresser." She was just tired. Tired and apparently in need of some downtime with her yoga mat. If she could find it. Or, even better, some fudge. The one thing she did not need was to think about this man's chest, his arms or the way he was scowling at her. "I was trying to move a table and lost my grip.

"So," she said, fully prepared to move on so he'd move himself.

He didn't budge. "Which table?"

Trapped between the counter, bins and boxes, she leaned sideways and pointed toward the eight-foot-long, solid oak-and-iron refectory table jammed between a bedroom set and the dairy case. "That one."

His scowl deepened as it swung back to her. "You tried to move that yourself?"

"It wasn't going to go inside on its own."

Forbearance entered his tone. "You said you were going to wait for the kids who moved you here to help with the heavy stuff."

"What I said," she reminded him, just as patiently, "is that they'd be back next week."

"When next week?"

"When they can fit it in."

"Meaning this could all be here a week from now," he said flatly. "Or the week after that."

She didn't particularly appreciate the cynical certainty in his tone. Especially since she was trying not to dwell on that discouraging suspicion herself.

"What about your friends?" he asked, clearly prepared to pursue other possibilities. "Have you asked any of them to help you?"

"I'm sure everyone's busy."

"Do you know that for certain?"

She could omit and evade. No way could she lie. Thinking of the few people she still thought of as friends, she muttered, "Not exactly."

"Then ask."

She started to say that she didn't want to. Fearing she'd sound like a five-year-old, not liking how he prodded at her defenses, she ignored the command entirely.

Since he had yet to move, she ducked around him. "I'll go turn on the heat."

She would do her best to cooperate with him for his help with the store. She could cut corners somewhere else to keep expenses down.

"I only took two bar stools inside, so there are a couple more back there we can bring up to sit on. I'm going to tell Tyler I'll be out here. He's watching a DVD on my laptop."

Erik watched her slip behind the counter, his focus on the resolute set of her shoulders as she disappeared inside. Her son was undoubtedly watching her laptop because her television was buried somewhere in the stacks beyond him. He also gave the guys she'd hired about a fifty-fifty chance of returning to finish their job.

He didn't care what she said. She did need help here. She just didn't want to ask for it.

Considering that she hadn't wanted to accept his little housewarming present, either, he couldn't help but wonder if the woman was always unreasonable, impractical and stubborn, or if some less obvious trait compelled her to refuse assistance when she clearly needed it.

What she needed now was some serious muscle.

Judging from the size of the decidedly upscale sofa and armchairs, sections of wall units, tables and a huge mirror sitting between the rows of shelving, there had been significant space in the house she'd left behind. The larger of two armoires was the size of a king-size mattress. He had no idea where she was going to put that. It might have fit in the largest of the bedrooms upstairs, but it would never make the bend at the top of the staircase.

He pulled his cell phone from his pocket, checked the time before scrolling through his contact list.

He'd just ended his call when she hurried back through the door.

"I have a friend on the way to help with the heavy stuff," he announced. "You and I can take care of the rest of it." Pushing up his sleeves, he motioned to an overstuffed, roll-armed, oatmeal-colored chair blocking a bedroom set. "Where does that go?"

Beneath a dusting of dark hair, his forearms were roped with sinew and muscle. They looked every bit as strong as she imagined them to be, but it was his left arm that had her staring. A silvery scar, hook shaped and wide, slashed from wrist to elbow.

"Just part of a collection. Caught a jib line when it snapped," he said, seeing what had her attention. "It couldn't be helped." His glance slid pointedly to the sore spot on her arm. "Unlike banging yourself up trying to move something you had to know was too heavy for you.

"So where do you want it?" he asked. "The living room?"

His presumption made her let the table reference go.

"You don't need to do this." *Part of a collection,* he'd said. He had more injuries like that? "And you definitely didn't need to call your friend."

Unease over what he'd done had collided with a hint of concern for the scar. Or maybe what he saw was embarrassment warring with interest. Whichever it was, he could practically see her struggling to decide which should take precedence as she moved with him toward the chair. The process, he thought, was rather fascinating.

"Yeah," he muttered, undeterred. At least she now had some color in her cheeks. "I did. I can't get those dressers up the stairs by myself."

"I meant, you didn't need to impose on him at all. I can't ask you to do this," she stressed, only to have him hand her the chair's seat cushion.

"You didn't ask," he pointed out.

"You know what I mean," she muttered back, arms wrapped around the awkward bulk.

"What I know is that there's no way to go over the inventory when we can't even get to it. So, yeah. I do need to do this." Challenge lit the chips of silver in his steel-gray eyes as he pulled one of her arms free and handed her the wide back cushion, as well. His glance slid to her biceps. "You're skinny, but you have more muscle than I'd thought. This'll go faster if you help."

Over the tops of the pillows, Rory could have sworn she saw challenge shift to a smile. Too disconcerted by him and what he'd done to stand there and make certain of it, she turned with the cushions and headed for the door.

She'd admit to having lost a couple of pounds in the past year or so, but no one had called her skinny since sixth grade.

"Which room do you want the twin bed in?" she heard him call.

"The one next to the master," she called back.

She had no intention of arguing with him. Not just because she didn't want to appear difficult. Or because he had a valid point about not being able to get to the inventory. As unsettled as her life felt—would always feel, she feared—getting the visible chaos under control would be huge. Tyler having his own bed that night would be nice, too.

Focusing on her son distracted her from the man carrying up her little boy's bed. For all of five minutes. The moment Tyler saw his bookshelf going up the stairs, he wanted to help. Wanting to keep him out of Erik's way, since she was trying to stay out of it herself, she waited until the piece was in place, then put him to work filling the shelves with his toys. While Erik moved on to tackle the living room furniture, she carried in lamps, pictures and, now that she could get to it, her box of potted herbs for the kitchen windowsill.

They didn't work together so much as they worked around each other. Erik clearly just wanted to get the job done so he could get on with the job he was there to do. Hating how she'd inconvenienced him, she just wanted to get it done, too.

An hour later, she'd returned to the base of the stairs for the rolled-up dinosaur posters she'd left there when muffled male voices drifted from inside the store.

"No way is this thing going up the stairs," she heard Erik insist. "Not without a saw."

"She might take exception to that," came the sensible reply. "How about through the bedroom window? Aren't there picture windows on that side of the house?"

"We'd have to take the window out and bring over a

crane, but it might be doable. The boys could load the EZ-Rig on a trailer and one of them can drive it over."

"That would do it." The unfamiliar voice paused. "There just isn't enough time to do it today. Not if you want the rest of this cleared out. That party starts at six."

Not totally sure what had the men talking about bringing in heavy equipment, equally concerned by mention of a prior obligation, Rory left the posters and poked her head inside the store. In the bright overhead lights, she saw Erik facing the large cherry armoire that blocked one of the grocery aisles. He stood in profile to her, his arms crossed over his broad chest, his wide brow furrowed.

He seemed totally occupied with logistics. She just couldn't see whom he was talking with. Whoever it was remained hidden by the sizable piece of furniture.

Needing to remove the apparent complication, she scooted past the checkout counter. "If it can't be carried up, just leave it. Or move it out of the way if you need to. I'll figure out what to do with it later."

Erik's glance caught hers as an athletic-looking male in worn denims and a plaid flannel shirt stepped from behind the armoire. The man had a scant inch on her mentor in height, which put him in the range of six-three or so, and the same imposing, broad-shouldered, leanly muscular build that spoke of intimate familiarity with hard physical work. Or a gym.

Beneath his wavy, wood-brown hair, his eyes narrowed an instant before he smiled. That smile seemed as easygoing as the man himself when Erik introduced him to her as Pax Merrick.

"My business partner," Erik added.

Pax reached out. "And partner in crime."

Shaking her hand, he gave her a quick once-over, the kind men who enjoy women often do, along with a rakish wink. "We go back a long way. You're Rory," he said, sparing his partner the introduction, along with whatever he could have added about their apparently extensive history.

Her glance bounced between the two unquestionably attractive, undoubtedly successful, probably rather fearless males. With the sense that their history might be rather intriguing, she offered Pax an apologetic smile of her own. "I'm really sorry to cut into your day like this."

"Not a problem. He'd do the same for me," he admitted, eyeing her with no small amount of curiosity. "You're really taking over this place?"

Something in the man's tone gave her pause.

"I am," she replied. "Why?"

"It'll seem really different, is all. I used to hang out here with Erik when we were kids. We built our first boat in Gramps's garage down there. And this store... It was just the Sullivans here all those years. They had sort of a mom-and-pop thing going," he explained, looking her over as if to verify some preconceived impression. "Down-to-earth. Comfortable, you know? I never thought about it being run by someone…"

Like you, she was sure he'd been about to say, only to be cut off by the quick-but-subtle slicing motion Erik made across his own throat.

"…else," he hastily concluded. "But if Erik's going to teach you the ropes," he hurried to add, "I'm sure you don't have a thing to worry about. The guy's got the patience of Job."

Meaning he thought she was going to require…what? she wondered, swinging her glance to Erik. Patience of biblical proportions?

Erik pointedly ignored her. "Are you going to help me move this, Merrick?"

"Absolutely. I'm on it."

As if wanting to muffle his partner, Erik motioned to the furniture the large piece blocked. "As soon as we get this out of the way, we'll take up your son's dresser," he told her. "Where do you want those bookcases?"

"In the spare room across from Tyler's." *Please,* she might have added, but his friend's insinuation still stung.

"Is there a bed that goes in there?"

"I don't have a spare bed anymore." She nodded toward the headboard and nightstands an aisle over with the same carving as the armoire. "That's a set we had in a guest room. I'll use it for my room now."

She'd sold the bed she'd slept in with Curt for so many years. Its new owner had picked up all the master bedroom furnishings the morning her movers had come. She'd sold the bulk of her other possessions to an estate broker she'd met at the country club to which she no longer belonged. Had it not been for Tyler, she'd have sold everything and bought only what she'd need to start over. But too much had changed for him already for her to indulge the need she felt to shed all the reminders of a life that no longer was.

Taking a deep breath, she pushed her hand through her hair and looked over to see Erik still watching her.

"I take it you've downsized."

"You have no idea," she murmured back.

She couldn't imagine what he saw in her expression, but she saw something in his that looked remarkably like understanding. It was as if he knew what it was like to walk away from the trappings and reminders of a former life. Whether he'd had no choice or the choice had been solely his, she had no idea. All she felt with any certainty as he shoved up his shirtsleeves to get back to work was that he wanted no part of those reminders now.

The realizations gave her pause. As she turned away herself and headed inside to pick up the posters, so did her disquiet over his partner's unwitting revelations. The fact that Erik had obviously implied to his friend that she would require considerable patience was merely annoying. She also questioned just how patient he actually was, given his steamroller approach to getting her things moved out of his way. But what truly troubled her was what his friend had said about her mentor's grandparents having been there for so long.

She hadn't even considered what her neighbors and customers would think of someone new running a business that might well be some sort of institution in the area. She'd already been wondering if she could keep it open year-round, and added that to her list of questions for Erik. Her newly heightened concerns about fitting in she'd have to add later, though, when she wasn't busy keeping Tyler out of the way of all the testosterone hauling bedroom furniture up the stairs.

Every time they clamored up the stairs and down the hall with another piece of something large, he'd dart to the door of his new bedroom to watch them go by.

Pax joked with him, noticeably at ease with small children. Erik, preoccupied, said even less to him than when he'd been around him before. He'd given him a half smile on their first pass, which had put a shy grin on Tyler's face, then barely glanced at him at all.

Because her little boy continued to wait in his doorway for "the man with the boat," it soon became painfully apparent that Tyler was hoping Erik would acknowledge him again—which had her feeling even more protective than usual when he asked if he could help him.

"I don't think so, sweetie. They're in a hurry," she explained, brushing his sandy hair back from his forehead. "When people get in a hurry, accidents can happen."

"If I be careful can I help?"

Erik heard the tiny plea drift down the hallway. Focused on getting Rory's possessions out of the way of the inventory, he'd paid scant attention to the child other than to make sure he wasn't where he could get something dropped on him.

But now they needed tools. Deciding to save himself a trip and do something about the dejection he'd heard in that small voice, he called, "Hey, Tyler. Can you do something for me?"

A nanosecond later, little footsteps, muffled by carpeting, pounded down the hall.

Tyler appeared in the doorway of the master bedroom, shoving his hair back from the expectation dancing in his eyes. Rory was right behind him, unmasked concern in hers.

Erik crouched in his cargos, his forearms on his thighs, hands dangling between his knees. Behind him, Pax continued squaring the bed frame to the headboard.

Rory's glance fixed on his as she caught her son by his shoulders. "What do you need?"

Whatever it was, she seemed prepared to do it herself. She had mother hen written all over her pretty face.

"Let him do it. Okay?"

The little boy tipped his head backward to look up at his mom. "Okay?" he echoed. "Please?"

For a moment, she said nothing. She simply looked as if she wasn't at all sure she trusted him with whatever it was he had in mind, before caving in with a cautious okay of her own.

It didn't surprise him at all that, physically, she hadn't budged an inch.

"There's a red metal box at the bottom of the stairs," he said to the boy. "It has socket wrenches in it. It's kind of heavy," he warned. "Do you think you can bring it up?"

With a quick nod, Tyler turned with a grin.

"No running with tools!" Rory called as he disappeared out the door.

"'Kay!" the boy called back, and dutifully slowed his steps.

Caught totally off guard by what Erik had done, Rory looked back to the big man crouched by her bed frame. He was already back to work, he and his partner slipping the frame parts into place and talking about how much longer it would take them to finish.

Not wanting to be in their way herself, she backed into the hall, waiting there while Tyler, lugging the case with both hands, grinning the whole while, made his delivery.

When he walked back out of the room moments later, his expression hadn't changed. She couldn't remember the last time her little boy had looked so pleased. Or so proud.

"Erik said I did good."

She knew. She'd heard him.

"Can I show him my boat?"

"Maybe some other time. He's really busy right now," she explained, then added that *she* really needed his help finishing his room.

Helping his mom wasn't nearly the thrill of helping the guys. Especially when Erik called for him again ten minutes later, this time to carry down the tools he'd had him bring up.

From where she stood on a chair adjusting the ties on a primordial-forest curtain valance, she watched Tyler walk by his bedroom door with both hands again gripping the handle of the red metal box. Right behind him came Erik, telling him he'd take the box when they got to the stairs so he wouldn't lose his balance with it.

Right behind Erik, Pax paused and poked his head into the room.

"I've got to run, Rory. No need to stop what you're doing," he called, because she'd done just that. "We have a client's Christmas party tonight or I'd stick around and help. Erik's going to finish up."

She'd forgotten they had plans. Groaning at the lapse, she left the last tie undone and headed for the door.

Erik had disappeared into the store. Tyler, now empty-handed, stood in the entryway as Pax passed him, ruffling his hair on the way.

"What can I do to repay you?" she called.

"Do you bake?"

"What's your favorite cookie?"

"Any kind that goes with coffee." Grinning, he disappeared, too.

Erik eyed his buddy as Pax walked into the store. "If she has any spare time," he insisted, setting the toolbox on the counter, "she'll need to spend it out here."

"Hey," his shameless partner said with a shrug, "if she wants to bake me something, it'd be rude to refuse. So how much longer will you be?"

Erik flatly rejected the odd sensation that hit out of no-where. It almost felt like protectiveness. But just whom he felt protective of, he had no idea. The woman wasn't Pax's type at all. "Half an hour at the most."

"You taking a date tonight?"

"Yeah," he muttered, the word oddly tight. "What about you?"

"I'm leaving my options open. I'll cover for you if you need more time," he added, his smile good-natured as he headed out the store's front door.

Erik wished he'd left his options open, too. Though all he said to his partner was that he'd catch up with him at the party and turned back to what was left of his task.

The aisles were finally clear. The inventory visible. Except for the large armoire they'd moved to the empty space near the front door and the boxes and bins Rory had said she didn't need just yet, mostly those marked *Christmas*, nothing else needed to be carried in. Except for her monster of a dining table, which they'd put in place, he and

Pax had carried the rest of the furniture in and left it all wherever it had landed in the living room.

His briefcase still lay on the checkout counter's marred surface, its contents untouched.

Burying his frustration with that, he glanced up to see her watching him uneasily from the inner doorway. More comfortable dealing with logistics than whatever had her looking so cautious, he figured the furniture in the living room could be pushed or shoved into place. It didn't feel right leaving her to do it alone. It wasn't as if she'd call a neighbor for help with the heavier pieces. She didn't even know them. And she'd seemed inexplicably reluctant to call in a friend.

"Where do you want the sofa? Facing the window?" That was where his grandparents had always had theirs.

Rory wanted it to face the fireplace. She just wasn't about to impose on him any more than she already had.

"I'll take care of it," she insisted, because he had that purposeful set to his jaw that said he was about to get his own way. Again.

"What about the big cabinet?"

"It's fine where it is. For now," she conceded, not about to tell him she wanted it moved across the room to the stair wall. "I'm hugely grateful for your help with all this, Erik. And for your friend's. But I'd just as soon not feel guiltier than I already do for having used your time like this. You came to work on the business. Not to help me move in. You need to go now."

One dark eyebrow arched. "I need to go because you feel guilty?"

"You need to go because you have a date."

She'd obviously overheard his conversation with his partner. Not that it mattered. Like Pax's unveiled allusion to the care and feeding Erik had told him he was sure she'd require, nothing had been said that he'd rather she hadn't heard. He'd bet his boat she already suspected he wasn't crazy about being there, anyway.

"Right." He wasn't in the habit of leaving a woman waiting. "We'll get to the inventory later this week. I won't have time until Friday."

"Friday will be fine. I'll be here. And thank you," she added again, touching his arm when he started to turn away. The moment he turned back, she dropped her hand. "For letting Tyler help," she explained. "I haven't seen him smile like that in a really long time."

Thinking the cute little kid had just wanted to be one of the guys, he murmured, "No problem," and picked up the toolbox and his briefcase. There was no reason for her to be looking all that grateful. Or all that concerned.

Still, as he told her he'd call her later and turned for the door, adding, "Bye, sport," for the little boy who'd just appeared behind his mom, cradling a toy boat, he really wished he didn't have the date with the bubbly event planner he'd taken out a couple of weeks ago. He didn't know the striking blonde all that well, but she'd been easy on the eyes, into sailing and, had he been interested in pursuing her hints, not at all opposed to a little casual sex.

He just hoped she'd need to make it an early evening so there'd be no awkwardness at her door. His head wasn't into games tonight. He wasn't much up for a party, either, though he wasn't about to stand up a client.

For reasons he didn't bother to consider, what he wanted to do was stay right where he was.

Chapter Four

The last thing Rory wanted Friday morning was to be late for her meeting with Erik. Or for him to be on time.

As she turned her car into her gravel parking lot, she realized she wasn't getting her wish on either count.

She'd also just confirmed her suspicions about the gleaming white seaplane she'd seen tied to the dock at the bottom of the rise. It was Erik's. He was on her porch, leaning against a post.

The fact that her mentor flew his own plane meant that he hadn't had to queue up for the ferry or get caught in traffic the way she and the rest of the mortals had crossing the sound and navigating surface streets that morning. It also meant that it had only taken him minutes to make the flight that was now a ninety-minute-each-way expedition for her to Tyler's school.

Hating that she'd caused him to wait, she left her little car in the otherwise empty lot in front of the store rather than park it in her garage and hurried toward where he'd straightened from the post. "I'm sorry I'm late. I was the last car off the ferry," she called, praying he hadn't been there long. They'd agreed on eleven o'clock. It was only a few minutes after. Still… "How long have you been here?"

The ever-present breeze ruffled his dark hair as he pushed his cell phone into a front pocket of his jeans and picked up his worn briefcase.

"Long enough to figure out you weren't going to answer the back door or the one to the mudroom. I didn't realize you'd be gone. I was just going to call you."

His cloud-gray eyes slid from hers as a muscle jerked in his jaw. His skin looked ruddy from the chill. In deference to the cold, he wore a leather flight jacket—open, though, as if in defiance of the need for it.

She hadn't thought of him as defiant before. Or rebellious, or rash, or anything that might even hint at irresponsibility. He seemed too much in control of himself for that. Yet the finely honed tension surrounding him alluded to a sort of restiveness that implied far more than his impatience with her, and made her acutely aware of how restless a man with flying and sailing in his blood might be. Restless. Daring. Bold.

She couldn't remember the last time she'd felt anything that wasn't tempered by the numbness that lingered deep inside her. And she'd never felt bold in her life.

What she felt most was simply the need to keep pushing forward. Especially now. Forward was good. Looking back made it too easy to fall apart.

He didn't need to know that, though. As she crossed the porch planks, searching her crowded key ring for the unfamiliar key, she figured all he needed to know was that she would make this venture work. Exactly how she would do that was as much a mystery to her as the dawn of creation, but she figured the basics would be a good place to start. And basically, she knew she needed this man to help make it happen.

His footsteps echoed heavily as he came up beside her, his big body blocking the wind whipping at her hair. "Where's your son?"

"At school. He only has tomorrow and next week before winter break, so we're commuting."

"To Seattle?"

Conscious of him frowning at the top of her head, she tried to remember if the key she'd just selected was for the store's front door, its emergency exit, the door to the house or the side door to the garage.

"I don't want him to miss working on the holiday projects with the other kids. He already missed the first of the week because of the move and he really wants to help decorate the school's big tree." He wanted a big tree, too, he'd told her. A *huge* one. How she'd make *huge* happen currently fell in the mystery category, too. "Since he won't be going back there after Christmas, it's about the only thing keeping his mind off the need to change schools right now."

"How long does that take you?"

"An hour and a half, if you include queuing up for the ferry."

"You're spending three hours over and back in the morning, and another three hours every—"

"That's just today," she hurried to assure him. "I'll usually only make the round-trip once. Kindergarten is only four hours, so I'll run errands while he's there." And maybe see if she could slip into her friend Emmy's yoga class, since seeking calm seemed more imperative by the moment. "A friend is picking him up with her son this afternoon. He'll play at their house until I get there."

His tone went flat. "So you came all the way back just to keep this appointment."

"You said it was the only time you had this week."

"You could have told me you'd be in Seattle," he insisted. "I never would have expected you to come back here for this."

"You said we had to go over the inventory. We have to do that here, so there was no point in mentioning it."

The key didn't work. Her head still down, his disapproval doing nothing for her agitation, she picked out another.

Before she could try that one in the lock, Erik reached over and snagged the wad of keys by the purple rhinestone-encrusted miniflashlight dangling below them.

"That's to the garage." He paused at the practical bit of bling, chose one beside it. "You want this one."

He held a duller brass key by its blade.

"Next time something like this comes up," he continued, biting back what sounded a lot like frustration, "mention it."

All her rushing had left her jumpier than she'd realized. Or maybe it was the edginess in him that fed the tension she did not want to feel with this man. Taking the key, conscious of how careful he'd been not to touch her, she forced the hurry from her tone.

"My schedule is my problem, not yours. I'll make sure it doesn't interfere with what you need to show me here. Not any more than it has already," she concluded, since last time he'd wound up hauling in her furniture.

Trying not to give him time to dwell on that little failure, she slid the key into the lock.

As the lock clicked, he moved behind her. Reaching past her head, he flattened his broad hand on the heavy wood door.

His heat inches from her back, the nerves in her stomach had just formed a neat little knot when he muttered, "Then let's get to it," and pushed the door open.

Intent on ignoring the knot, disconcerted by their less-than-auspicious start, she hurried into the store to the warning beeps of the alarm system.

With the front display windows shuttered for the winter, the only light came from what spilled in behind them. Relying on that pale shaft of daylight, she headed straight for the checkout counter and the inner door behind it, mental gears shifting on the way.

Feeling his scowl following her, she deliberately sought to shift his focus, too.

"I'm going to start the coffee. While I do that, would you look over the floor plan I came up with? It's right here on the counter." Fluorescent lights buzzed and flickered as she snapped switches on. Punching the security code into the pad by the inner door, the beeping stopped. "I'll be right back."

In less than a minute, she piled her purse, coat and scarf onto the dining table, flipped on the coffeemaker she'd already filled and grabbed the tape measure she'd left on the island.

She'd barely turned back into the store when the hard line of Erik's profile had her freezing in the doorway.

He'd tossed his jacket over the far end of the U-shaped counter's now-bare surface. Without it, she could see *Merrick & Sullivan Yachting* discreetly embroidered in sky-blue on the navy Henley hugging his broad shoulders. Ownership, she thought. He had a definite sense of it. He had it stitched on his shirt. His initials, she'd noticed before, were on the latch of his briefcase.

On the scarred beige countertop lay the file she'd left open. His frown was directed to the new floor plan she'd come up with.

"You did this?" he asked.

With a vague sinking feeling she walked around to him. She might not know anything about the little doodads in the bins and on the Peg-Boards hanging in her new store, but she was a consumer with her fair share of shopping hours under her belt. If the interior didn't have some appeal, people might run in to buy what they needed, but they wouldn't stick around to browse and buy more.

"The store needs updating," she said simply, certain he could see that himself. "I thought it might make the space more interesting to have three shorter horizontal shelving units in back than that one long one down the middle. The floor space along here," she said, pointing to the front and back walls on the drawing, "would be a little narrower, but the endcaps would allow for ninety-six more inches of display space. I could use part of the longer piece—"

"I'm not asking you to defend this," he interrupted mildly. "I'm just asking if you drew it."

Erik's only interest when he'd first arrived had been in tackling the task they hadn't even started the other day. As far as he was concerned, they were already behind schedule if she was to open in April. Not wanting to fall further behind and risk her not making a success of the business, he'd just wanted to get in, get out and get back to work until the next time he had to meet with her. It had been that ambivalent sort of annoyance eating at him when he'd realized what she'd done to accommodate him.

The trip by air between the store and Seattle was nothing for him. Minutes from takeoff to touchdown, depending on head- or tailwinds and whether he left from his houseboat on Lake Union or the boatworks in Ballard. The drive and a ferry ride for her was infinitely less convenient. People commuted from the inner islands every day. But she had actually come back from Seattle just to meet with him, and would have to return later that day to pick up her son.

Even the time it would normally take her on other days seemed an enormous waste of time to him. She was right, though. How she did what she needed to do was her problem. Just as it was his problem, not hers, that he didn't want to consider changing the store from exactly as it had been for decades.

The need to play nice so they could reach their respective goals wasn't what had his attention at the moment, however. It was the detail in the drawing. It hadn't been generated using a computer program. The floor plan had been drawn with pencil on graph paper. While the layout was admittedly simple, the measurements and identity of the elements were all perfectly drawn and precisely printed. It had the touch of a professional.

"Oh," she murmured, apparently understanding. "I took a drafting class a few years ago. We'd thought about building our own home and I wanted to understand what the architect was talking about." She gave a shrug, the motion nowhere near as casual as he suspected she intended it to be. "We never got to the blueprint stage, though. We bought instead."

We.

The freshness of her soap or shampoo or whatever it was clinging to her skin already had him conscious of her in ways he was doing his best to ignore. He'd caught the light herbal scent of her windblown hair when she'd pointed out the walls on the drawing. He caught it again now. Whatever it was she wore seemed too subtle to define. But the elements managed to hit his gut with the impact of a charging bull.

Telling himself he didn't need to know anything about her that didn't apply directly to his reason for being there, he deliberately overlooked her reference to the man she'd married—along with the subtle havoc she wreaked on certain nerves—and indicated a rectangle she'd drawn by the front door.

"So what's this?"

"That's the armoire over there. It just needs to be moved

back against that wall and down a few feet and it'll be perfect. A couple of neighbors stopped by to welcome me yesterday. Actually, I think they came to check me out," she admitted, because their curiosity about the "single woman who'd bought the store" had been so obvious. "But one of them mentioned that she makes organic soaps and creams. She has a friend up the road who makes candles for craft shows. I thought I'd see what else is made locally and put a gift display in it."

He eyed her evenly. "This isn't a boutique."

"Are you saying it's a bad idea?"

He wasn't going to commit to anything yet. He was still back on her having taken a drafting class just because she'd wanted to understand her architect.

"When did you do this?"

Realizing he hadn't shot her down, a hint of relief entered her eyes. "After Tyler went to sleep in the evening. And between 1:00 and 3:00 a.m."

Sleepless nights, he thought. He'd once been there himself. Having one's world turned upside down did tend to promote a certain degree of restlessness. He figured it didn't help matters that she was trying to sleep in an unfamiliar house, in a bed she apparently wasn't accustomed to, either. She'd said the one she was now using had been in a guest room.

The thought of her in bed, tossing, turning or otherwise, had him reaching for his old briefcase.

"Let's get to the inventory. Once you know what you have to work with here, you'll know what you need to order and how much shelving space you can actually use."

"So you think this floor plan might work?"

The layout of the shelves his grandfather had built had served its purpose effectively for years. Changing anything about it hadn't even occurred to Erik. The old-fashioned footprint of the place was simply part of the store's personality. It always had been.

He'd thought it always would be.

He gave a mental snort, blocking his reaction to the change as irrelevant. No one knew better than he did how transient "always" could be. The store was hers now, he reminded himself yet again. She was free to do anything she wanted as long as she could turn a profit.

"It might. Probably," he conceded, because her plan would certainly better define the grocery section from the sporting goods. Using the big armoire to promote local artisans wasn't a bad idea, either.

Still, there was no denying the reluctance in his agreement. He could practically hear it himself. He also couldn't help but notice the small smile Rory immediately stifled.

It pleased her to know that her first instincts and efforts toward her new business were good ones. It didn't feel good to him, though, to know he'd deprived her of sharing that pleasure with the only person available. He was her mentor. He was supposed to be encouraging her. Showing a little enthusiasm.

Before he could tell her just how good her instincts probably were, she'd crossed her arms over the glittery designer logo on her hoodie and moved on.

"Before we start the inventory," she prefaced, "would you tell me about the customs your grandparents had here? One of the ladies I met said she hoped I'd have a farmers' market on the porch like the Sullivans did every summer. The other one said that the Harbor Market lighted walking kayak was missed in the Chimes and Lights parade last week."

She hadn't realized such an object even existed until Edie Shumway, the fortysomething community volunteer and, Rory suspected, neighborhood busybody, had explained what it was. Apparently Erik's grandfather and one of his cronies from the local lodge provided propulsion for the Christmas-light-covered kayak—which explained the two holes she'd finally noticed in the bottom of the one hanging from the ceiling in the back of the store.

"I'm going to call the lodge and see if I can get a couple of volunteers to walk it in the parade next year. I'll provide candy for them to throw to the kids, and get elf hats like Edie said they wore. But I need to know what else your grandparents did that I should do, too."

Erik hesitated.

"I'm not totally sure what you're after."

"Anything they did for holidays, or for community events. Or things they did every year that people looked forward to."

"Like the kayak and the elf hats," he concluded.

"Exactly. I want to belong here," she explained, as if that need meant as much to her as financial success. "I want us to fit in. The other day, your friend implied that this place was sort of an institution around here. If there are customs your grandparents had that their neighbors and customers looked forward to, then I'll keep them up the best I can."

"You want to maintain my grandparents' traditions?"

"If you'll tell me what they were."

Erik was not a man who impressed easily. Nor was it often that a woman caught him so off guard. Even as the businessman in him commended her approach to public relations, a certain self-protectiveness slipped into place.

Resting one hip on the counter, he crossed his arms over his chest, conscious of her honest interest as she waited for whatever he might be willing to share.

"They always gave suckers to the little kids." A few innocent memories would cost him nothing. And possibly help her bottom line. "And ice cream bars. Locals always got a free one on their birthday." His grandma had kept a calendar under the cash register with the regular customers' birthdays written on it. Anniversaries were there, too.

He told her all that, ignoring an unwanted tug of nostalgia as he began to remember traditions he'd taken for granted, then forgotten. Or noticed but overlooked.

"They always opened the week of the spring sailing regatta in April, so they hung nautical flags along the porch and a life preserver by the door. For the Fourth of July they hung bunting and handed out flag stickers," he said, memories rushing back. He'd loved the Fourth as a kid. Lying on his back in the grass to watch the fireworks over the sound. Or better, being out on the water in a boat, watching them explode overhead.

"And every fall," he continued, thinking her little boy would probably like it, too, "the porch would be full of pumpkins and hay bales and they'd serve cups of cider."

With her dark eyes intent on his, she seemed completely captivated by the small-town customs he hadn't considered in years. She also appeared totally unaware of how close she'd drawn to him as he spoke. As near as she'd come, all he'd have to do was reach out and he would know for certain if her skin felt as soft as it looked.

As his glance slid to the inviting fullness of her bottom lip, he wondered at the softness he would find there, too.

Her lips parted with a quietly drawn breath.

When he looked back up, it was to see her glance skim his mouth before her focus fell to his chest and she took a step away.

"What about Thanksgiving and Christmas?" she asked, deliberately turning to the file on the counter. "Aside from the kayak."

Forcing his attention back to her question, he stayed right where he was.

"Thanksgiving was just the fall stuff. But the day after, Gramps would string lights along all the eaves and porch posts and set up a Christmas village with a giant lighted snowman." There had been a time when he and his dad had usually helped. That was back when Thanksgiving dinner had always been here. Christmas had been at his parents' house, around the bend and in town a couple of miles. After the aircraft company his dad worked for had transferred him to San Diego a few years ago, he'd headed south for that particular holiday.

"The store was closed for the season by then, so I don't think they gave anything out. At least, not the past several years." He hadn't been around to know for sure. Seattle was only twelve miles as the crow flew, but he lived his life what felt like a world away. Unless his grandparents had needed something before they'd moved south, too, he'd given this place and the areas around it as little thought as possible. And he'd never given it as much thought as he had just now. "But a lot of people drove by to see the light display."

Whatever self-consciousness she'd felt vanished as she glanced back to him. "Where are the lights now?"

"They were sold."

"The snowman, too?"

"Everything. They had a garage sale before they moved."

For reasons he couldn't begin to explain, he wasn't at all surprised by her disappointment. What did surprise him was that he actually felt a twinge of it himself.

"Tyler would have loved to have a big snowman out there," she said. "And the village. He gets so excited when he sees Christmas decorations."

Threading her fingers through her hair, she gave him a rueful smile. "Unfortunately, I'd thought I was moving somewhere a lot smaller, so I sold everything for outside except a few strings of lights."

With the lift of her shoulder, she attempted to shrug off

what she could do nothing about now, anyway. "What else is there I should know?"

From the pensiveness in her voice, there wasn't a doubt in his mind that she was still thinking about how her little boy would have loved what his grandparents had done.

"I can't think of anything right now." Wanting to get her mind off what she couldn't do for her son, and his thoughts off her mouth, he rose from his perch. "But if I do, I'll let you know."

"One more thing," she said as he turned to his briefcase. "Everything I've heard so far tells me this will be a good place to live. But what do you think about it? The community, I mean."

Just wanting to get to work, he opened the case with the snap of its lock. "It is a good place. I grew up in town, but I was around here a lot, too. I even came back after college." Paper rustled as he pulled out a sheaf heavy enough for a doorstop. "Pax and I first went into business about a mile down the road." The stack landed on the counter. "You and your son should be fine here."

Considering that Erik had apparently lived much of his life there, it seemed to Rory that the entire area had to mean a lot to him. "Why did you leave?"

He pulled another stack of paper from his scarred briefcase. For a dozen seconds, his only response was dead silence.

"Didn't your business do well?" she prompted.

"The business did fine."

"Then if this is a good place to live and your business was doing well, why did you go?"

The defenses Erik had attempted to ignore finally slammed into place. He knew her question was entirely reasonable. It was one he'd want answered himself were he on the other end of their agreement. Yet as valid as her query was, it bumped straight into the part of his life that had led to an entirely different existence than he'd once thought he'd be living by now.

His plans had been unremarkable, really. No different from half the guys he knew: a good marriage, build boats, a couple of kids, maybe a dog. The one out of four he did have was 90 percent of his life. It was a good life, too. The rest he'd written off completely years ago.

"It has nothing to do with here."

"What did it have to do with, then?"

"Nothing you'd need to be concerned about."

"How can I be sure of that if I don't know what it is you're not telling me? If you were getting your life established here," she pointed out, "it's hard for me to imagine why you'd leave. You seem too much in command of yourself and everything around you to do that if you'd really wanted to stay. That's why your reason for leaving is important to me." She tipped her head, tried to catch his glance. "Was this place lacking something?"

She'd stated her conclusions about him more as fact than compliment. As if she saw his influence over his surroundings as basic to him as his DNA. He'd have been flattered by her impression of him, too, had it not been for how much control he'd actually given up to save the marriage that had ultimately ended anyway. He could see where she deserved something more than he'd given her, though. After insisting his business had been fine there and that she would be, too, he did feel somewhat obligated to explain why he hadn't stuck around himself.

"It didn't lack for anything," he admitted. At least, it hadn't as far as he'd been concerned. "I left because my ex-wife wanted to teach in the city for a few years before coming back to raise a family. Those few years led to a few more and she changed her mind. About coming back and about the family," he admitted, making a long story as short as possible. "When we left here, the business had barely gotten off the ground. But by the time I realized we weren't coming back, Pax and I were established in Ballard. We had a good location. We had good people working for us. So it made sense to stay there. Like I said, my leaving had nothing to do with anything around here."

Thinking he'd covered all the bases, he added two more stacks of papers to the first.

"She was a teacher?"

"Kindergarten," he said without looking up. "She was great with kids."

Her voice went soft. "You wanted children?"

A folder landed on the pile. "Let's get to this, shall we?"

He'd said as much as he was going to. He'd closed the door on all the excuses Shauna had come up with to delay having a baby, and on how he'd hung in there because he'd promised to be there for better or worse. She'd kept asking him to bear with her on the baby thing. Especially after his business took off. She'd eventually changed her mind about a baby, but only after they'd divorced and she'd remarried. He'd realized then that it wasn't that she hadn't wanted children. She just hadn't wanted his. She'd had no problem, however, keeping the house and a hefty chunk of their assets.

Frowning at his thoughts, he turned the whole stack of what he'd unloaded toward Rory. The past was just that. Past. Over. Done.

Rory saw a muscle in his jaw jerk.

The demise of his marriage evidently hadn't been his choice.

She thought that an incredibly sad thing to have in common. She'd had no choice in hers ending, either.

"I'm sorry about your wife."

"Ex."

"Ex-wife," she corrected. She spoke quietly, feeling bad for having pushed, worse for what she'd discovered. He'd once had plans to build his life in the fiercely beautiful surroundings where he'd grown up, but circumstances had forced him to move away, and move on. Just as circumstances had forced her in an entirely different direction than she would have chosen, and led her to the very place she strongly suspected he truly no longer wanted to be.

"Marriage can be complicated," she said, beginning to appreciate the roots of his restiveness. "That must be why it's never easy no matter how it ends."

The furnace kicked on with the rattle of the floor vent behind the counter. His head down, his hand on the printout, Erik slowly ruffled a corner of the pages with his thumb.

He'd heard understanding in her voice, suspected he'd see it in her fragile features were he to look up. She seemed to think they shared the same kind of pain.

He didn't want that kind of sympathy. He didn't want to poke around at what he'd finally grown so far beyond, or into what was undoubtedly fresher and more painful territory for her. And he definitely didn't want to be as curious as he couldn't seem to help being about her, or the man she'd married. She'd once spoken of her child's loss. There'd been no doubt in his mind at the time that she hurt for her son. He just hadn't considered how the boy's pain could easily compound the depth of the loss she felt herself.

Mostly, though, he didn't want her getting so close, or to get close to her. Emotionally, anyway. Physically would be just fine. Heaven knew he was aware of her in ways he had no business considering. But she didn't seem anything like many of the women he knew, those looking for a good time, no commitments involved. Not that he'd been intimate with anyone in longer than he cared to remember. He didn't want any commitments, either. Still, he'd grown tired of the games, the shallow conversations and walking away feeling little more than...empty.

He gave the top folder a nudge. "I'm sorry about yours, too," he admitted, because he didn't need to know the details to feel bad for her. "And you can have a good business here," he assured, because it was his job to help her make that happen. "We just need to get to work so we can make sure of it.

"This is my grandfather's business plan," he said, opening the folder. "Since you're new to all this, it'll be your bible. We can tweak it as we go, but to get you up and running, it'll be simpler not to deviate from it too much at first. This—" he pulled the top printout forward "—is a stock list of the groceries they kept on hand, divided by type and vendor. Dairy, produce, snacks, staples, that sort of thing.

"This printout," he said, indicating the tallest stack of paper, "is your sporting goods department. There are certain vendors you'll need to order from weeks or months in advance. Others can ship in twenty-four hours. You'll want to get their new catalogs. Gramps said they're all online, but some will mail hard copies. You'll need to establish accounts in your name with all of them."

He handed her a CD. "It's all on here for ordering and bookkeeping purposes. Look through it, list your questions and we'll go over them later. I want to get you started on the physical inventory. You need to know what you have on hand, so it's as good a way as any to get your feet wet."

The change of subject was as subtle to Rory as the slam of a door. He would share anything that would help her make a success of the business. But his personal life was now off-limits. Despite how deftly he'd closed off his past, however, he'd revealed wounds that might well have taken years to heal. Family mattered to him. His dreams had mattered. Once.

She'd give anything to know how he'd survived knowing that the woman he'd married had no longer loved him.

For her, even harder than Curt's death was the knowledge that he might not have ever loved her at all.

The deep tones of Erik's voice somehow overrode the sick sensation that inevitably came with the thought. Or maybe it was simply his no-nonsense presence that managed to keep that awful feeling at bay.

"We can start with things you can probably identify even if you've never used them. Camp stoves, lanterns, backpacking gear," he said. "Or go with something that might be more of a challenge. Your choice."

He was there to teach her what she needed to know to reopen the store, not about how to live with questions that could now never be answered. From his deliberate allusion to her lack of knowledge about certain outdoor activities, she had the feeling, too, that he intended his baiting to pull her out of her thoughts. If not for her sake, definitely for his own.

Since he had far more experience with both the store and self-survival, the least she could do was follow his lead.

"More of a challenge."

He said he wasn't surprised.

First, though, she brought them each a cup of coffee, his black, hers with milk, which they took with a section of the printouts and a notepad to the back of the store. It was there that he told her he needed to leave by two o'clock, which, thankfully, was a few minutes before she needed to leave to catch the ferry to pick up Tyler. So for the next hour, she learned to identify lures, hooks, rods, reels, creels, the difference between a bobber and a sinker and the different weights of leader—which would be important to know, he told her, if a customer came in asking for twenty-pound test. At least now she'd know they were asking for fishing line.

"If someone wants fish, wouldn't it be a whole lot more convenient to buy it from a grocery store?"

Towering beside her, he remained focused on a column of item numbers. "Might be convenient, but it wouldn't be nearly as much fun."

"I take it you've never been to Pike Place Fish Market." She focused on a page of her own. "You pick out the fish you want and the guys behind the cases toss it down the line to the scale. You get it wrapped, packed, you don't have to gut it and the show is free. That's fun enough for me."

With that even-eyed way he had of looking at her, he slanted her a tolerant glance. "You're missing the point."

"The point being?"

"Being in the great outdoors. The thrill of landing a thirty-pound salmon, or pulling an eight-pound rainbow trout from a freshwater stream."

"The guilt of taking Nemo from his mother," she muttered.

"What?"

"Never mind. I doubt that you know him."

"Please tell me that's not the approach you're going to take with your customers," he muttered back, just before his glance dropped to her mouth—which had the odd effect of shutting her up and getting her back to verifying counts.

They didn't have time to move on to the modest sections of hiking, camping or boating equipment before she noticed the time. Since she had to drive right past the marina at the end of the street, and he'd tied his floatplane there, she asked if she could give him a ride and save him the two-block walk in the misty rain.

Conscious of the time himself, he told her that would be great. She could go over the rest of the inventory on her own and call him with any questions. They'd meet again next week after she'd gone over the business plan. He also asked if he could take the drawing of her new floor plan with him.

Thinking he intended to give the layout she wanted some thought, she handed it over, along with a travel mug of coffee since he seemed to like hers. Minutes later, he'd just tossed his briefcase into the back of her fuel-efficient little car and folded his big frame into the passenger seat when her cell phone chimed.

One glance at the caller ID had her bracing herself an instant before she dropped the phone back into her bag, started the engine and backed up. The phone continued to chime as she pulled onto the wet two-lane road and headed down the rise.

Erik's glance cut from her purse to her profile.

"I'll call her back," she said. "It's Audrey. My mother-in-law. She's calling about plans for Christmas." The woman was actually returning Rory's call, something it had taken her three days to do. The conversation would be short, but it wasn't one she wanted to have with Erik in the car.

"She *was* my mother-in-law," she corrected. Technically, Rory was no longer related to the Linfields. Audrey had apparently pointed that out to Lillian Brinkley, the wife of the country club president, who had ever so thoughtfully shared it in the ladies' room with two other members of the socially connected among the mourners at Curt's funeral. Rory had been seeking a few minutes of quiet while closed in a stall at the time.

According to Audrey, via Lillian, Rory's vows with her son had been "until death do them part." They'd parted, however sadly. End of legal relationship.

As strained as her relationship with Curt's parents had always been beneath the polite manners and civility, Rory hadn't doubted the remarks at all.

"She's really only Tyler's grandmother now." That was the only part that mattered, anyway.

The wipers swiped at the heavy mist on the windshield. Through the veil of gray, the little marina came into clearer view. Erik barely noticed. For a couple of hours he'd caught glimpses of a woman whose guard with him had begun to ease, a smart, savvy woman who possessed no small amount of determination, ingenuity and a remarkable willingness to step beyond her comfort zone.

What he saw now was a woman doing her level best to mask disquiet. He'd seen her do it before, for her son's sake. Her attempts seemed to work fine on her five-year-old, but Erik recognized strain when he saw it. With her eyes on the road, he watched her take a deep breath, slowly ease it out.

Whatever was going on with Tyler's grandmother had her hands going tight on the wheel.

The heater whirred in its struggle to produce warmth, gravel crunching beneath the tires as she pulled to a stop by the wooden stairs that led to the long floating dock. In the choppy, chill water of the sound, his white Cessna Amphibian floated and yawed where he'd secured it at the end of the pier, well away from the few sport boats moored there this time of year.

He almost always felt better flying from this place than toward it.

"Thank you for your help today," she murmured, her hands now tucked at her waist, her shoulders hunched against the still-cold air. "I'll come up to speed on everything as fast as I can. I promise."

The bravado behind her smile pulled at protective instincts he'd rather ignore. He knew she wanted to belong there, in a place she'd known absolutely nothing about until last week. He knew she wanted to make a good home for her son. He suspected, too, that she could use a little reassurance on both counts.

After all, she was pretty much on her own here.

"I'll pass that on to our benefactor," he promised back, wanting to keep his purpose there in perspective. "And for what it's worth, Rory, you and your son really should do well here." He hesitated, perspective faltering. "I'd always thought it was a good place to raise a child."

He reached for the door, cold salt air blasting in as he opened it. "I'll call you next week. In the meantime, call me if you have questions." He climbed out, then ducked his head back in to retrieve his case from the backseat. "Thanks for the ride."

Rory had barely opened her mouth to tell him he was welcome before the door closed. In the space of a heartbeat she'd swallowed the words and was staring at his broad, leather-covered shoulders as he headed for the weathered stairs.

He'd made it halfway down the dock, his long stride sure and certain despite the drift and roll beneath his feet, when she finally put the car into gear. Even with the surface beneath him shifting with the unpredictable current, the man seemed as steady as a rock.

I'd always thought it was a good place to raise a child.

The admission had cost him. She felt as certain of that as she did of her gratitude for his having shared it. He knew his opinion mattered to her. She'd told him so herself. But sharing that particular thought had also demanded a hasty retreat back to the world he now lived in, back to a world so different from what he'd once wanted.

What stung, though, wasn't how anxious he'd been to retreat to the life he'd created for himself. It was the sharp, undeniable feeling that he had quite deliberately retreated from her.

Chapter Five

Rory returned the call to Curt's mother within a minute of dropping off Erik at the dock. When Audrey didn't answer, she left a message saying she was sorry she'd missed her and asking her to please call back as soon as it was convenient.

Despite two other attempts to reach her, it apparently hadn't been "convenient" for four days.

The conversation they'd had still had Rory reeling three hours later. Thanks to the distraction a text from Erik provided, however, at that particular moment she didn't have to struggle to mask the resentment, offense and indignation she wasn't about to impose on her little boy, anyway.

"Is Erik at our new house now, Mom?"

Following the beam of her headlights through the steady rain, she murmured, "Probably, honey."

"Can I help him again?"

"We'll have to see. I'm not sure why he's coming."

The text she'd received from Erik that morning hadn't given her a clue.

Am in mtgs. Need to know if you will be home around 6.

She'd texted back that she'd be there by 6:15 p.m.

His reply had been a wholly unenlightening See you then.

Since he'd indicated he'd be in meetings, she hadn't called to see what he wanted. She hadn't talked to him at all since he'd closed her out at the dock last week, even though he'd told her to call if she had any questions.

She had dozens. Between online catalogs and searches, she'd figured out the answers to most of them, though, and talked herself out of contacting him about the rest. Those she simply added to her list to ask at their next meeting. Partly because they weren't urgent. Mostly because she suspected that what she really wanted was more of the relief she'd so briefly experienced when he'd assured her that she and Tyler would be all right. The sensation hadn't lasted long enough to do much more than tease her with the hope of finding the security she hadn't truly felt in forever, but she desperately needed to feel something positive about the more personal aspects of her life—and that wasn't something she should be seeking from him at all.

There also existed the unnerving little fact that she'd just wanted to hear his voice—something she insisted she shouldn't even be thinking about, considering that she was nothing more than an obligation to him.

That glaring bit of reality mingled with her turmoil over her in-laws as she turned onto the gravel drive just past the store. Through the silvery drizzle, her headlights illuminated a black, bull-nosed pickup truck loaded with something large covered in plastic.

She'd barely pulled into the garage and gathered her

groceries from the backseat when Erik strode up and plucked the heavy sack from her arms.

"Anything else back there?" he asked.

Raindrops glistened in his dark hair, beaded on his leather jacket. His impersonal glance swept her face, his brow pinching at whatever it was he saw in her expression.

Not about to stand there trying to figure out what that something might be, she turned away. "Just one bag. I can get it."

Ignoring her, he reached into the car as Tyler raced around the back bumper and came to a screeching stop.

One strap of his green dinosaur backpack hung over his shoulder. The other dangled behind him as he looked up with a shy "Hi."

Erik straightened, looking down at the child looking up at him. "Hi yourself, sport."

Anticipation fairly danced in her little boy's hazel eyes.

As if unable to help himself, Erik smiled back and held out the bag of apples he'd snagged off the seat. "Do you want to take this?"

At Tyler's vigorous nod, he waited for the child to wrap his arms around the bag, then nudged him toward the warmth of the house. With Tyler doing double time to match Erik's long strides, Rory punched the remote to close the garage door and hurried to catch up, clutching her shoulder bag and keys.

She couldn't believe how pleased Tyler looked to see him.

"Were you on the ferry?" she asked, torn between her son's growing fascination with the man and trying to imagine why he was there.

"I took the long way around. I had a meeting in Tacoma," he told her, speaking of a town at the south end of the sound, "so I drove. Jake was on it, though. He should be right behind you."

"Jake?"

"One of our craftsmen." Rain glittered through the pool of pale yellow light that arced from the neat back porch. Even in that spare illumination, Erik could see strain in the delicate lines of her face, could hear it in her voice. "I'll explain when we get inside."

He watched her hurry ahead of him. Her head down, she unlocked the door and ushered Tyler inside, reminding him to wipe his feet on the way.

The mudroom, with its pegs for coats, cabinets for storage and the double sink his grandmother had used for repotting plants, opened into the kitchen. The warmer air held the same welcome it always had, but no longer did it smell of the pine disinfectant his grandmother had used with abandon when mopping the floors. Now lingering hints of lemon soap gave way to scents of cinnamon and orange as Rory distractedly flipped on lights and told him to set the bags anywhere.

The island of the neatly organized kitchen seemed as good a place as any. As he set the bags on the laminate surface, his glance cut to where she'd left on a lamp at the far end of the long, open space.

She'd just moved in last week, yet everything appeared to be in order. Furniture had been pushed, pulled or shoved into place. Drapes and pictures were hung. Not a box remained in sight.

Not a hint of what had once been familiar remained, either.

The walls had been bare for over a year. Having walked through that empty space a dozen times, it no longer felt strange without the chaos of floral patterns and knick-knacks his grandparents had acquired living there. But with that blank canvas redecorated, the sense he'd had the other day of no longer belonging there, of having lost a piece of himself, threatened to surface once more. He didn't doubt that it would have, too, had the unexpected ease of what she'd created not distracted him from it.

The well-defined spaces now bore his student's decidedly understated stamp. The heavy wood pieces he'd carried in were dark and substantial enough to make a man feel comfortable, but balanced by shades of ivory and taupe that felt amazingly...restful.

The rustic refectory table with its high-backed chairs held a large pewter bowl filled with glittered pinecones and cinnamon potpourri. Beyond it, the deeply cushioned sofa faced the stone fireplace at the end of the room. A long, narrow sofa table behind it held a trio of thick cream-colored candles. The two armchairs he'd brought in had been positioned to one side, a heavy end table stacked with books and a chrome lamp between them.

He turned to see that she'd left her raincoat in the mud-room. The apples and her shoulder bag had landed on the desk by the now child's-art-covered refrigerator—mostly red-and-green construction paper bells. Sinking to her heels in front of her little boy, she worked his jacket's zipper.

"You've been busy."

Oblivious to what had his attention, conscious only of his presence, Rory understated considerably.

"A little," she replied, thinking of the day she'd had and how desperately glad she was for it to be nearing its end. "I had a meeting with the probate attorney." Now that the house had sold, she'd had more paperwork to sign. "And I had to go to the bank to close the safe-deposit box, then go straighten out my medical insurance."

The good news was that she could pay the attorney's fees and increased insurance costs from the proceeds of the sale of the house. The not so good part was that both cost more than she'd expected—which meant she'd have to forgo the new sign and new shelving she'd hoped to have for her store's grand opening. And buy a considerably smaller Christmas tree than a version of the megadollar, floor-to-ceiling noble fir that had so mesmerized Tyler at his school. She'd already ruled out buying more outdoor lights to pay for the ferry rides.

Budget concerns, however, had taken a backseat to the varying degrees of anger and hurt she'd been busy stifling all afternoon. Thanks to Curt's mother.

"After I picked Tyler up from school," she continued, "we dropped off library books and went grocery shopping before we caught the ferry."

"And saw Santa ringing a bell at the store," supplied Tyler, still in Christmas mode. "Not the real Santa," he explained. "Mommy said he was a helper." He gave a sage little nod. "The real Santa has lots of helpers."

"Be tough to do all he does alone," she explained. Her little boy's zipper now freed, she rose and headed for the bags. "I hope the milk stayed cold."

Erik had never seen her in a suit and heels before. A crisp white blouse peeked from beneath the black jacket that curved at her waist and hugged the hips of her slim pencil skirt. Black tights covered the long, shapely line of her legs. As he glanced up from her spike-thin heels, he had to admit he hadn't seen her truly upset before, either. Though she definitely was, and trying hard to hide it.

"I meant you've been busy around here."

Apparently realizing the extent of her preoccupation, she met his eyes and promptly closed hers with a sigh.

"Can I have an apple?" Tyler asked.

She forced herself to brighten. "You'll ruin your appetite, sweetie." Taking his head between her hands, she kissed the top of it, hard, and tipped his face to hers. "Hang up your jacket and empty your backpack. Dinner will be ready in a few minutes."

With Tyler dragging his jacket into the mudroom, she reached into the nearest bag to unload groceries. She'd just put the milk in the fridge and grabbed two boxes of cereal when she turned on her stylish heel.

The boxes landed on the counter three feet from where Erik watched her with his hands in the pockets of his cargos. The stance pulled the sides of his jacket back from the navy pullover covering his chest and made his shoulders look broad enough to bear the weight of the world.

It seemed terribly unfair just then to be taunted by the memory of how very solid his chest had felt. Especially when she so badly wanted to be held against it. But fair hadn't been a big part of her day.

"I'm sorry." She shook her head, the neat wedge of her hair swinging. "You didn't drive all the way here to watch me put away groceries." She tried for a smile. "May I get you something? Juice? Milk?" Neither sounded very adult. "Coffee?"

He took a step toward her. "I didn't come to interrupt. I just want to drop off your shelving."

"My shelving?"

"The three units for the back of the store. I had a couple of the guys work on them with me over the weekend. With Christmas coming, they were up for the overtime. One of the units is in the back of my truck. Jake is bringing the rest."

Disbelief cut through the anxiety that sat like a knot beneath her breastbone. They'd barely discussed her layout to update the market. Though he'd said it would probably work, he hadn't even bothered to tell her whether or not he liked the idea. All she'd done was show him her sketch, explain why she wanted it and all of a sudden the shelving she'd felt certain would now have to wait had materialized. He made it happen just like that, as if he was some sort of...fairy godfather.

The man fairly leaked masculinity. As utterly male as he was and so *not* fatherly in the way he'd checked out her legs, the thought would have made her laugh had she not felt like crying.

"You made my shelves?"

"You wanted them, didn't you?"

She wanted world peace, too, but that didn't mean she expected it to happen.

She raked her fingers through her hair, wondering if they were a gift, which she couldn't accept without reimbursing him. Wondering, too, how much he'd paid his men, since it was undoubtedly more than she could afford.

"Yes. Absolutely. I'm just…" *Speechless,* she thought. "Thank you," she concluded, because she had no idea what else to say before the ring of his cell phone had him pulling the instrument from his pocket.

After two short beeps and a glance at the text, he muttered, "Jake's out front," and dropped the phone back into his pocket. "I'll be back in a few minutes. Then you can tell me what's wrong."

Certain he was referring to her less than gracious reaction, she said, "Nothing is wrong. You just caught me off guard. I never expected you to make the shelves—"

"I meant what was wrong with you when I got here."

Oh. That.

Thinking him far too astute, uncomfortable with that, too, she turned for the cereal. "It's nothing."

Moving with her, Erik stopped scant inches from her back. With Tyler just around the corner, he lowered his voice to nearly a whisper. "Lying is a bad example to set for a child."

Conscious of his warm breath moving her hair, her head still down, she lowered her voice, too. "Then how about it's nothing I can talk about in front of him?"

"That's better." Taking a step back, he indicated the door near the stairway. "I need to get into the store. Mind if I go in through the living room?"

Since he tended to do what he wanted to do anyway, she was a little surprised that he'd asked. Mostly, she was just conscious of how close his muscular body still was to hers. All she'd have to do was turn around…

She shook her head, swallowed hard. "Not at all."

"Give me half an hour. I'll be back."

Twenty minutes was actually all the time it took him and his employee to unload the sections of the three shelving units from a company vehicle and the back of Erik's truck. It wasn't long enough, however, for Erik to question why he couldn't leave well enough alone with the woman he'd spent the past few days trying not to think about at all. Not beyond her needs for the store, anyway. He'd told her to call him if she needed anything. Since she hadn't, he'd assumed she was doing fine.

Except she clearly was not. Even when he let himself back inside, greeted by the scent of something delicious, there was no mistaking the disquiet she was still trying to hide.

Tyler smiled from where he sat on the dining room side of the island. Beyond him, light glowed through the glass-paned white cabinets, revealing neat stacks and rows of plates and glasses.

"Mom's making mac and cheese. It's my favorite. You want some?"

"Mom" had shed her jacket and heels. She stood across from them in her stocking feet, stirring a pot on the stove. The cuffs of her white blouse had been folded back. A green dish towel had been tied into an apron at the waist of her skirt. Erik knew she'd heard him come in, but it was her son's innocent invitation that had her looking over her shoulder with apology in her expression.

"I told him you probably already had plans," she said,

sounding as if she fully expected his refusal and had already prepared her son for it. "But he wanted to ask anyway."

Had this been any other woman, any other child, Erik knew without a doubt that he'd have done what she obviously expected and come up with some excuse for not being able to stick around for dinner. With just the three of them, the beat of the rain against the windows and the cozy warmth of the kitchen countering the cold outside, the scenario felt entirely too domestic for him.

He wanted to know what had upset her, though. If for no reason other than to be sure it wouldn't impede her progress with the store. Or so he told himself. He also knew she wasn't going to say a word about whatever it was as long as her son was present.

Then there was the little boy himself. With Tyler looking all hopeful, he simply didn't have the heart to say no.

"Mac and cheese, huh?"

Again, the quick nod. "It's really good."

"Then I guess I'd better stay." He looked to the woman at the stove, caught the strain countering the softness of her smile. "That okay, 'Mom'?"

Her hesitation held uncertainty, and collided with something that looked suspiciously like gratitude for indulging her child. "Of course it is. Tyler?" she asked. "Let's move your place mat to the table and get another one from the sideboard for Erik."

Erik tossed his jacket across the stool next to where Tyler sat. As he did, the boy scrambled down and grabbed his pine-green place mat from the island. Intent on his mission, he laid it on the heavy oak table, then pulled a matching one from a long drawer in the printer's cabinet his mom had pushed to the wall by the stairs.

He'd just set the mat across from the other when he looked back to the man tracking his progress. "Do you want to see my boat?"

Erik hadn't a clue what had prompted the question. Seconds ago they'd been talking about food. With a shrug, he said, "Sure," and the little boy was off.

Wondering if the kid's energy ever ran low, he walked over to where Rory spooned dinner into two shallow pasta bowls.

"What can I do?" he asked.

"You've already done it," she said quietly. "He's wanted to show you that boat ever since you said you build them. After you told him about the boats outside Cornelia's office, it was nearly all he talked about." She turned, a bowl in each hand. "But if you want, set these on the table for the two of you while I slice another tomato. That would be great."

Handing them over, she slipped past him to take two salad plates from the cupboard.

"Where's yours?"

"I'm not hungry. What do you want to drink?" she asked, pointedly avoiding his scrutiny as he set the bowls on the table.

Walking toward them with his toy, Tyler announced that he wanted milk.

Rory told him she knew he did. As she set salads of tomatoes, herbs and olive oil above their place mats, she also said she knew he really wanted to show Erik his boat, but right now he needed to sit down and eat his dinner before it got cold.

She appeared as calm and unruffled to Erik as he'd always seen her with her son. Still, he recognized restlessness when faced with it. There was no mistaking the nerves that had her too keyed up to sit down herself. She seemed to be using motion as a means to keep that tension under control as she started pulling measuring cups, flour and a big wooden spoon from cabinets, cupboards and drawers.

Intimately familiar himself with the cathartic effects of

movement, specifically his usual morning run or sanding teak until his arms ached, he said nothing about her joining them. While she moved about the kitchen side of the island, he turned his attention to the boy who'd docked his little blue plastic boat on the table between them.

His fork in his fist, Tyler stabbed a noodle. "It's my Christmas boat."

It certainly was.

The miniature ski boat held a hunk of clay middeck. A peppermint-striped straw stuck up from the little blob like a mast. More clay anchored a bit of pencil-thin neon-green tinsel from bow to mast and mast to stern.

He'd rigged the tinsel on it just like the lighted boats they'd talked about in Cornelia's office.

Erik couldn't believe how deeply touched he was by the boy's innocent desire to share something of his with him. Or how humbled he felt by the innocent expectation in the child's eyes.

The silence coming from the table had Rory nearly holding her breath as she waited for Erik to acknowledge what her son had shared.

He finally picked up the toy, turned it in his big hands.

She could have hugged him when he said, "Now that is one awesome sailboat."

Tyler beamed.

Rory felt her heart squeeze.

Setting the child's handiwork back on the table, Erik pointed his fork at the bow. "Do you know what that's called?" he asked.

"The front?"

"That, too," came his easy reply. "But in nautical terms, the front of a boat is called its bow."

"What's 'not-cul'?"

"Nautical," Erik emphasized with a smile. "It means things relating to boats and sailors," he added, which led

Tyler to ask what the back was called. That led to a discussion of stern, port, starboard and keel, the latter of which his ski boat didn't have, but which Erik fashioned out of a paper napkin just so Tyler would get the idea of what one looked like.

When Rory casually mentioned that she was going to have to reheat their dinner if they didn't start eating, conversation turned to the merits of shell-shaped pasta over elbow while they cleaned their bowls. Over pudding for dessert, talk then turned back to the boat—specifically the differences between sail and motor.

Her child ate up the attention her mentor so generously bestowed while she put cranberry muffins into the oven to have with breakfast and cleared their dishes. By the time she'd finished cleaning up the kitchen and removed the muffins from the oven twenty minutes later, it was nearing Tyler's bedtime, and she didn't want to impose on Erik any further.

"It's time to put the boat away," she finally told him. "Say good-night to Erik now, okay? And go brush your teeth. I'll be up in a few minutes to tuck you in."

She'd thought he would do as she'd asked and simply say good-night. Instead, with his toy under one arm, he walked to where Erik stood by the island and wrapped his free arm around the man's thigh. "'Night, Erik," he said.

She wasn't sure who was caught more off guard by the unexpected hug—her or the man who went completely still a moment before his big hand settled on Tyler's head.

"'Night, sport," he murmured back. "Thanks for showing me your boat."

Tyler tipped back his head, gave him a smile. "You're welcome."

Her conversation with her former mother-in-law already had Rory's maternal instincts on high alert. Torn between allowing the draw her child obviously felt toward someone who would be out of their lives in a matter of months and the need to protect him from it, she took him by his little shoulders and eased him back.

"Teeth," she reminded him, and turned him around to get him headed in the right direction.

"Can I read?" he asked on his way.

"Until I get there," she called after him.

"'Kay," he called back and disappeared up the stairs.

"He's a neat kid." The admission came almost reluctantly, as if he hadn't wanted to be as impressed—or touched—as he was by a five-year-old. "I don't know how long it's been since he lost his dad, but you seem to be doing a great job with him."

It had been fourteen months that sometimes felt like mere weeks. Sometimes, strangely, as if it had been years.

"It was a year ago in October. And thank you," she offered at the compliment. "Thank you for being so nice to him, too. I'm sure you had other things to do tonight, but you just made his week. He's not around men very often," she said, compelled to explain why her son had monopolized his evening. "And he really misses his dad."

"I imagine he does." The agreement brought a frown. "What about relatives? Grandfathers? Uncles?"

She shrugged. "My parents are in Colorado." This month, anyway. Heaven only knew where they'd be this time next year. "I'm an only child. So were my parents. So that's it for my side. Curt's family is in Seattle, but his parents aren't...available." Pushing her fingers through her hair, she could practically feel the hurt building in her chest. Even with Tyler out of earshot, her voice sank at the heartlessness of what had been said. "Actually," she conceded, "they don't want anything to do with him."

He took a step closer, his brow dropping right along with his voice. "Why wouldn't they want to see their grandson?"

The need to restrain her resentment pushed hard. The

hurt pushed back. It was Erik's expression, though, the un-questioning disapproval in it, that urged her on.

"Until a few hours ago, I'd thought it was just because of me," she admitted, pride biting the dust. "I don't care about having a relationship with Curt's parents for myself. I gave up wanting their acceptance a long time ago. But they're family. Tyler's, anyway," she clarified, reminded again of how succinctly her change in status had been pointed out to Audrey's friends. "For his sake, I did want him to have a relationship with them. I wanted him to have traditions.

"Especially this time of year," she hurried on. "Curt and I barely had time to start our own and my parents never had any." None that counted, anyway. None she wanted to pass on. "But as much as anything, I'd hoped he'd have a sense of being part of more than just him and me."

This wasn't the first time she'd mentioned traditions to him. The last time he'd been there, she'd made learning those his grandparents had maintained over the years a huge priority. But discovering why she apparently lacked those bits of history herself—and, if he had to guess, the sense of belonging that came with sharing them—would have to wait. He was far more interested in what had her looking agitated enough to pace the walls.

Until a few hours ago, she'd said.

"Does this have something to do with that call from his grandmother when you dropped me off last week?"

It had everything to do with it. It also surprised her that he remembered it.

"I finally talked to her this afternoon. I already knew she didn't want me to be part of their Christmas Day," she told him, hating how she'd even let that matter to her. "But I'd hoped I could stop by for an hour or so with Tyler on Christmas Eve so he could spend some time with them. Audrey hadn't sounded thrilled with the idea when I first asked," she admitted, understating considerably, "but she'd said she'd get back to me. She called while I was on my way from the lawyer's to pick up Tyler at school."

Rory would be forever grateful that Tyler hadn't been in the car at the time. She had known for years that the senior Linfields hadn't approved of her. She'd just had no idea until that call how little they'd cared about the child their son had so dearly loved. "She and Curt's father decided it best that there be no further contact between us. She said it was just too painful for them to see me or 'the boy.'"

The hurt she felt for her son shadowed her eyes, filled her hushed voice as slights of past years could no longer be ignored.

"I should have seen this coming." She turned toward the rack of muffins cooling on the counter. Turned right back. "Nothing about this ever came up while Curt was alive, but since his death they haven't wanted to spend any time with Tyler at all." Twice she had arranged to meet them. Once for Curt's father's birthday so Tyler could give him the present he'd made for him, a collage of photos of Tyler and his dad. Once for a trip to the zoo. Both had been canceled by last-minute calls from Audrey. "I'm just glad I hadn't told him we'd be seeing them at Christmas. It's so much easier on him to not get his hopes up at all than to have him be disappointed all over again."

She turned back to the muffins, brushed a couple of crumbs from the counter into her palm, took two steps to the sink.

"What are you going to tell him if he asks about seeing them?"

"I don't know. I haven't had time to figure that out."

"Maybe they'll change their minds."

With a glance toward him, the crumbs landed on white porcelain.

"Only if you believe in hell freezing over."

The rush of water in pipes told her the child under discussion remained occupied in the upstairs bathroom. Still, her voice grew quieter as agitation had her turning away, turning back once more.

"Audrey said that they feel no bond with him." She spoke bluntly, as Audrey had. "That they never have. She said they tried while Curt was alive, for Curt's sake, but with him gone, there was no need to keep up the pretense. He's not their son's blood, so they want nothing to do with him. Apparently, they already amended their will to delete Curt's 'legal offspring.' Heaven forbid 'the boy' should get a penny of their precious money."

Caution crossed the hard angles of Erik's face.

"Not their son's blood." He repeated her words slowly, as if to make sure he hadn't misunderstood. "He's not Curt's child?"

As upset as she was, as insulted and offended as she was for her son, that caution barely registered. "Not biologically. We adopted him. We've had him since he was two days old," she explained, going with the bonds that really mattered. To her, anyway. "We didn't know until after a year of trying that Curt couldn't have children. It wasn't anything we ever discussed with anyone," she added in a rush. "We just said that the opportunity to adopt came up and we couldn't say no. After nearly four years and no other children, I'm sure his parents figured the problem was with me.

"Not that it matters," she muttered, hugging her arms around her waist. "And not that I'll ever tell them otherwise. They hadn't liked me the minute they found out I was Curt's secretary and not a lawyer myself. You could actually *see* them withdraw when they found that out. It got even worse when they found out my 'people' weren't the right pedigree. But Tyler's a *child*," she insisted, only to forget whatever else she'd been about to say when she realized all that she'd said already.

Erik looked as if he wasn't about to interrupt her. Though one dark eyebrow had arched significantly, at which detail she couldn't be sure, he was clearly waiting for her to continue.

Appalled by the scope of personal detail she'd just dumped at his feet, she closed her eyes and turned away. Rubbing her forehead, she muttered, "I cannot believe I just told you that."

His hand curved over her shoulder. The comforting weight of it barely registered before he turned her back around.

"Which part?"

"About Curt's…"

"Inability to father a child?" he asked when her voice drifted off.

She gave a nod, not at all sure how she felt having divulged something that, until moments ago, had been only between her, her husband and their fertility doctor. She felt just as uncertain about the odd sense of loss that came as Erik's hand slid away. "And about how his parents felt about me."

He didn't seem terribly interested in that. "Curt was a lawyer?"

Of all the questions he could have asked, he'd gone straight for what had been so hugely important to the Linfield family status. "Corporate. His father's a litigator."

"His mother?"

"She's into charities."

"What about brothers, sisters?"

"A brother. He took after their dad. His life is the firm and his wife is from money. She and Audrey adore each other."

"So they had a problem with you not being equal, or whatever the hell it was?"

Among other things, she thought, though she wasn't

about to get into everything she'd overheard in that bathroom stall before she'd opened the door and watched Audrey's friends go pale.

She'd said more than enough already.

"Seems so," came her embarrassed agreement.

Quick, assessing, his glance swept her face. As if looking for where the problem might lie, apparently finding nothing in what he knew of her, utter certainty entered the low tones of his voice.

"Then this is their loss. Not yours." Lifting his hand as she lowered her head, he caught her chin with one finger, tipped her head back up. "And for what it's worth, everything you've said stays right here." He brushed the back of his finger along the curve of her cheek, only to catch himself and still the motion scant seconds later. Drawing back, he settled both hands on his hips. "All of it."

At the gentleness in his touch, her shoulders had risen with her indrawn breath. They now fell with a soft "Thank you" that had as much to do with his unexpected defense of her as his assurance that her secrets were safe with him.

She couldn't deny how good his support felt. She was also rather horrified by how badly she wished he would stop looking at her as if he wanted to touch her again, and just do it. She felt terrible for her child. Totally powerless to give him the family he'd once had, imperfect as parts of it had been. Knowing what she knew now, she didn't want him around the Linfields anyway. Yet what made her ache the most just then was what Erik had so inadvertently done.

Simply by touching her, he'd reminded her again of how long it had been since she'd been held. There had been brief hugs at Curt's funeral, many of them awkward, most of them part of the blur that awful time had become. She couldn't remember the last time she'd felt any measure of comfort from a man's touch. She couldn't even remember the last time she'd been in Curt's arms. Or the last time they'd made love. She could easily recall the last kiss Curt had given her, though. She'd played it over a thousand times in her head. As rushed and preoccupied with work as he'd been in the mornings, it had been little more than his customary peck on her cheek on his way out the door.

After what she'd overheard, she couldn't think of that kiss without wondering if it hadn't been tolerance more than preoccupation underlying those absentminded good-byes. But the awful possibility that the man she'd adored had merely endured living with her had existed since the day she'd buried him.

She shoved back the memories, fought the threatening ache.

"This is so not what you signed on for, Erik." She shook her head again, tried to smile. "Thank you for listening. And for your help. And for the shelves. I still can't believe you did that. Just tell me what I owe you." She'd add it to what she owed him for the oil. "And thank you for having dinner with my son," she hurried on, because that had been huge. "I'm sure you'll think twice about sticking around for a meal in the future, but if you do happen to stay, I'll make a point of not burdening you with my baggage."

Despite her attempt to brush off the pain of what she'd shared, she looked as fragile to Erik as the thin silver chain resting below the hollow of her throat. He didn't want her thanks or her money. What he wanted was more detail, not less. He especially wanted to know what she felt about the man whose privacy she still protected. He didn't question why that mattered to him, or ask anything about Curt now. He was too busy hating how the man's family had rejected her and the child she clearly cherished.

He'd never have guessed Tyler was not biologically her own. He'd just figured the boy had come by his fairer coloring from his father.

"What I signed on for was to make sure you can make

a success of the business. I'll do what I have to do to make that happen. I'm not taking your money, Rory. The shelves are just part of the service."

He could see her protest forming even as he lifted his hand to her cheek once more. It was as apparent as her disquiet that she didn't want to feel more obligated to him than she already did. Yet that protest died as he curved his fingers beneath her jaw and touched his thumb to the corner of her mouth.

"As for your son, he doesn't need people in his life who don't appreciate him." Having made her go still, he drew his fingers toward her chin. "And you have too much else to do to waste any more energy on people who don't appreciate you, either. Got that?"

She swallowed, gave him a small nod. Other than that questionable agreement she simply stood there, looking very much as if she was afraid to move for fear that he would.

He'd been physically aware of her since the moment they'd met. Knowing she wanted his touch made that awareness tug hard. She looked very much as if she needed to be held. Needed to be kissed. It was that stark vulnerability that drew him as his hand cupped the side of her face.

Lowering his head, he brushed his lips over the soft part of her mouth.

He heard her breath catch, felt it ease out, the warmth of it trembling against his cheek.

Rory wanted to believe it was just anxiety catching up with her as she slowly leaned toward him. Longing curled through her, a subtle yearning to simply sink into the incredible gentleness in his touch and let it take away the ache in her chest.

But that ache only grew.

So did the need for him to make it go away.

She leaned closer, drawn by that need, by him. As she

did, his fingers eased through her hair, tipping her head and causing her to cling a little more tightly, to kiss him back a little more deeply.

It was kissing him back that turned the ache to something less definable. Shattering sweetness gave way to confusion. She craved the feel of this man's arms, his strength, his self-possession. She just hated how needy she felt, and how badly she wanted him to make all the hurts and the doubts go away.

The pressure of her nails pressing into her palm suddenly registered. So did the realization that all that kept them from cutting into her flesh was the fabric wadded in her fists.

Beneath his own hands, Erik felt tension tightening the slender muscles of her entire enticing body. Before he could ease back himself, she'd released her death grip on his sweater and ducked her head.

Her quiet "I'm sorry" sounded like an apology for everything from the desperation he'd felt building in her to the way she'd bunched the front of his pullover. To remove any possible wrinkle she might have left, she hurriedly smoothed the fabric with the palm of her hand.

As if suddenly conscious of her palm on his chest, or possibly the heavy beat of his heart, she jerked back her hand and stepped away.

Erik moved with her, canceling that negligible distance. There wasn't a doubt in his mind that he'd just added to the chaos of all she was struggling with. That hadn't been his intent at all. Not totally sure what his intention had been, feeling a little conflicted himself, he lifted her face to his.

"Hey. It was just a kiss," he murmured, attempting to absolve them both. Just a kiss that had done a number on his nervous system, he qualified, but her decidedly physical effect on him was beside the point. "No apology necessary. Okay?"

Unlike her unease, her nod was barely perceptible.

"I'll call you in a couple of days." Aware of how she barely met his eyes, he consciously lowered his hand. He shouldn't be touching her at all. "Can you finish the inventory by Friday afternoon?"

As segues went, he knew his was positively graceless. All he wanted at the moment, though, was to get past the awkwardness that had her protectively crossing her arms as she pulled composure into place.

"I'll have it finished."

A wisp of her shiny bangs had fallen near the corner of one eye. Instincts that still wanted physical contact with her had him starting to nudge it aside. More prudent senses had him dropping his hand an instant before the small voice coming from the top of the stairs would have had him dropping it anyway.

"I'm ready to tuck in, Mom."

She took another step away. "I'll be there in a minute," she called toward the stairs. Brushing at the taunting wisp, she looked back with an uncomfortable smile. "He has to be up early in the morning."

"Then I'll get out of your way so you can take care of him. I'll let myself out," he said, stopping her as she started for the door. "Just say good-night to him for me."

His jacket lay on the stool behind her. Reaching around her, careful not to touch, he snagged it and backed up. "Thanks for dinner," he added, and walked out the mudroom door, wondering what in the hell he thought he'd been doing when he'd reached for her in the first place.

He had no one but himself to blame for the tension that had his entire body feeling as tight as a trip wire. He was messing where he had no business going. Even if she wasn't so obviously not the sort of woman a man could have a brief, casual affair with, she was just now moving on from a loss that had affected her in ways that went far beyond anything she'd shared with him.

He couldn't even pretend to understand how she felt, or to know what she needed. Whatever it was, he couldn't give it to her anyway. He didn't know how. Even if he did, he suspected she wouldn't let him close enough to try. She didn't want to rely on anyone she didn't absolutely have to. He could appreciate that. He'd been there himself. As it was there were only a handful of people he truly trusted— and not one of them was a female he wasn't related to or who wasn't in his employ. He suspected, though, that her walls weren't nearly as thick as those he'd erected around his heart. There was no denying how vulnerable she was right now.

He wasn't about to take advantage of that, either. He also wasn't going to do anything else to potentially screw up his relationship with her as her mentor and jeopardize his agreement with Cornelia.

That was why he'd told his lovely protégée that he'd call in a couple of days instead of meeting with her. If he wasn't near her, he wouldn't be tempted to touch.

That didn't stop him from being touched by her, though. Or by the little boy who'd strung Christmas tinsel on his toy boat.

He knew Rory wanted her son to have traditions. Knowing how tight her money was, and how badly she wanted this season to be special for the child, he decided there was no reason he couldn't give them one of the traditions that had long belonged there anyway.

Chapter Six

She never should have said she'd have the inventory finished by Friday. She should have asked for another day at least. As much as she required his expertise, she'd just made it a point to accommodate Erik's schedule any way she could.

Had she been thinking, she would have realized how impossible that deadline was. But she'd been too rattled by the needs she'd felt in his arms and the kiss he'd dismissed as inconsequential to consider everything else she'd committed to do before Friday—which happened to be Tyler's last day at his current school.

Given the occasion, guilt over not having kept her word to Erik would have to wait. Her little boy was not taking this latest transition well at all.

The familiar faces and routines at Pine Ridge Day School were the last constants in the life they were leaving behind. As a child, she'd had considerable practice dealing with such separations. Her parents' nomadic lifestyle had made a new school or two every year her norm, and they'd tried to ease those transitions. But her little boy had never known that sort of instability. Even after his father had died, she'd managed to protect him from the biggest upheavals and keep his routine as consistent as possible. Until they'd had to move, anyway.

As she'd feared he would, he started missing his playmates the minute he'd fastened himself into his car seat in the back of their car and they'd pulled out from the portico.

A quick glance in her rearview mirror caught his pensive expression. He looked the way he had driving away from their old house a couple of weeks ago. Solemn and a little uncertain.

"We can always come back for a visit, Ty," she assured him, heading for the freeway and the ferry. "Just because you'll be going to a new school doesn't mean you won't ever see your old teachers or classmates again."

"They'll still be there?"

"They'll still be there," she promised. It wouldn't be like when he'd lost his dad. There wasn't that sort of finality to this parting. She needed him to understand that. "We can come back after the holiday to say hi, if you want."

"Will the tree be there, too?"

The tree. Ten feet of pine studded with a thousand white lights and draped with paper chains and cutouts of students' handprints. It graced the main building's foyer.

"The tree won't be there, honey. Everyone takes Christmas trees down after the holiday. But everything else will be the same."

"Nuh-uh," he replied, picking at the knee of his khaki uniform pants. "I won't be there anymore."

No, she thought with a sigh. He wouldn't be, and the silence that followed hinted at how very much that new change disturbed him.

Thinking the Christmas carols playing on the radio

might distract him, she turned the volume up over the hum of the heater and encouraged him to sing along.

That didn't work. Neither did any of her other attempts to console, cajole or otherwise ease away his dispirited expression.

Fighting discouragement herself, she finally conceded that she had no idea just then how to make everything better for her little boy.

That disheartening fact had just registered when her eyes widened on what should have been nothing more than the dusk-gray shapes of the road, the woods and the distant rectangle of Harbor Market & Sporting Goods.

Peering past the headlights, she heard Tyler's sudden "Oh. Wow!"

Wow, indeed.

The market stood glittery bright in the encroaching dark. Every pillar, post and eave, its roofline, even the chimney had been outlined with twinkling white lights. The bare branches of the apple tree at the near end had been wrapped in peppermint stripes of white lights and red. It was the snowman beyond it, though, that had her attention. Glowing blue-white, his top hat cocked at an angle, the tall, grinning Frosty stood as bold and impressive as the only person she knew who would have put it there.

The light on her answering machine was blinking when she finally coaxed Tyler out of the cold and into the kitchen. Hitting Play, she heard Erik's recorded voice say he was checking to see if she'd finished the inventory and ask when she'd be available to discuss the business plan. He mentioned nothing about the dazzling Christmas lights that hadn't been there when she'd left that morning.

She hit Redial. Apparently taking his cue from the number on his caller ID, he answered with an easy, "You're home."

"We just got here. Erik," she said, her tone half laugh, half hesitation, "I can't believe what you've done."

"Is that good or bad?"

"I don't know." She honestly had no idea how to weigh her son's reaction against her next electric bill.

"Does Tyler like it?" he asked while she figured it out.

"Like it?" *This is* ours, *Mom?* he'd asked, his eyes huge. "He hasn't stopped grinning since we got here. He's practically stuck to the window right now watching the icicle lights."

The sequential lights strung along the overhangs looked like dripping ice. Even the back of the house had been decorated. They'd noticed the lights wrapped around the side of the building the moment they'd driven up the rise. "He loves the snowman."

"You said he would have liked the one my grandparents had," he reminded her over the drone of what sounded like an electric saw. "My grandfather always put theirs facing the sound, but I had it put farther back on the lot, thinking Tyler could see it from the window."

Truly torn by what he'd done, she dropped her scarf on the phone desk and unbuttoned her coat. When they'd talked about his grandparents' traditions with the store, he'd seemed to see maintaining them mostly as a good approach to business. Yet her mentor's gift clearly had less to do with marketing than with the little boy pressing his nose to the glass.

She didn't want his thoughtfulness to mean so much. She just wasn't able to help it. Not with her little boy so totally captivated.

"How did you get it done so fast?"

The drone beyond him grew quieter. Nearer, voices rose, then faded.

"This close to Christmas, lighting companies are usually finished putting up decorations and are just waiting to take them down. I called a company a client uses, told them what I wanted, gave them the building measurements and they did their thing."

Just like that. With one phone call, he'd managed to do what she hadn't been able to do no matter how hard she'd tried and totally distracted her son from his dejection.

"It's just lights, Rory."

The man had a serious gift for understatement. He'd used the same think-no-more-of-it tone right after he'd proved that the shell of control she fought to maintain around her life was about as thin as paper.

It was just a kiss, he'd said.

He was only being kind when he'd reached for her. Just as he was only being kind when he'd overlooked how she'd practically crawled inside his shirt when she'd kissed him back—shortly before he'd pointedly minimized the moment of comfort, security and whatever else she'd felt in his arms.

He, on the other hand, apparently hadn't felt much of anything at all, other than anxious to get out of there.

But this wasn't about them. Not that there *was* a them, she insisted to herself. This was about what he'd done for her child.

"It's more than lights, Erik. To us, anyway." He had to know that. "And Tyler loves them." That was all that she would let matter at the moment. For her son's sake, she wasn't even going to panic over the electric bill. Yet. "So thank you. From both of us."

"You're welcome. Listen," he continued over the thud of heavy boots on metal stairs, "I have to get back to the payroll right now, but we need to discuss your business plan and address inventory. I have to be in Tacoma before noon tomorrow, so let's do it over the phone. Are you okay for an eight-thirty call? That'll give us a couple of hours.

"You there?" he asked when she hesitated.

"Can we make it Sunday?"

"Sunday's not good for me."

"Actually," she began, wondering if Sunday involved the woman he'd taken out last week, "I'm not quite finished with the inventory." She hated telling him that. "I'd have finished last night, but we had to bake cookies."

With the bang of a door, the noise and conversations beyond him died.

"*Had* to?"

"I told Tyler's teacher I'd bring treats for his class today. And I'd promised him he could help. So, yes," she insisted. "I had to."

She'd also brought cookies for the staff—which meant she'd spent the past two afternoons and evenings baking and filling tins and decorating twenty-two gingerbread girls and boys. With Tyler's help, the project had taken twice as long as it might have, but she'd wanted something for him that she'd never had as a child, holiday memories of flour on noses, sugar sprinkles, the air scented with vanilla and spice. Her mom's idea of baking had been heating a muffin in the microwave.

"What about tomorrow? Will you have it finished by then?"

Juggling guilt and priorities, she rubbed the ache brewing beneath her forehead. "I told Tyler we'd get our tree tomorrow. I'm going to work in the store tonight after he goes to bed," she explained, hoping to minimize the delay to Erik's schedule. "After we get the tree decorated, I'll finish whatever I haven't done in the store. I've been working out there after he goes to sleep, but I ran out of hours in the past couple of days.

"Since Sunday isn't good for you," she hurried on, easily

able to imagine a scowl etched in his too-handsome face, "I'll be ready Monday for sure." That would also give her time to read the business plan she'd tried without much luck to study on the ferry and after Tyler had gone to bed. Having to look up terms like *gross margin, inventory turns* and *marketing mix* had also slowed her down considerably. So did being so tired her eyes blurred.

She hated the plea that entered her quiet "Okay?"

Leaning against the edge of his desk, Erik stared past the schematics on his drafting table to the black-framed photos of Merrick & Sullivan racing sloops lining the pearl-gray wall. To his left, the windows of his office, like those of the other offices lining the catwalk, over-looked the production floor a story below. Those on his right exposed the lights of other industrial buildings lining the night-darkened waterway.

The pleasure he'd felt knowing the snowman had been a hit with Tyler had rapidly faded to something far less definable.

When he'd left her place the other night, his only thoughts had been about doing what he could to make the kid's Christmas a little better, and his need for physical distance from the boy's mom. He'd wanted to focus on his work and his world and to get her out of his head for a while. He was good at that. Focusing his thoughts, his energies.

He usually was, anyway. His days were crowded enough to prevent more than a fleeting thought of her undeniably feminine shape, or the way her bottom lip curved when she smiled. But she was messing with his nights, too, driving him from his bed to pace the floor or exhaust himself with his weights before sleep would finally drive her from his mind.

He never should have kissed her. If he hadn't, he

wouldn't know the sweetness of her mouth, the feel of her satin-soft skin, how perfectly her body fit against his.

Now, frustrated on a number of levels, he pushed from his desk, jammed his fingers through his hair.

"Forget Monday," he muttered. Just because he would have preferred she keep her focus on his schedule didn't mean she could make it her priority.

In roughly two weeks she'd lost her job, sold her home and was settling into a place that hadn't even been on her radar until his amazingly generous neighbor had decided to help them both out. In between, she seemed to be doing everything she could to ease the transition for her son while dealing with the former in-laws from hell and getting a business she knew nothing about back up and running.

No way could he justify pushing her just because he wanted his obligations there over and done with.

"The store can wait for now. We'll pick up after Christmas."

Pure skepticism shaded her quiet "Seriously?"

"Seriously," he echoed. "You and Tyler have a good time picking out your tree. There's a great tree lot on Sydney Road. It's only a few miles from you. Old family operation. Tell them you bought John and Dotty Sullivan's store. I imagine they'll give you a good price on a little one."

"I'll do that. And thank you. Thank you," she repeated, sounding relieved beyond belief by the reprieve he'd offered. "But the tree can't be little. Tyler has his heart set on the tallest one we can fit into the room."

Erik's voice went flat. "The ceilings in there are nine feet high."

"Then I guess we're getting an eight-foot tree. That'll leave room for the angel."

"And you're hauling it how?"

"The only way I can," she replied, ever so reasonably. "On my car."

The thought of eight feet of freshly cut conifer atop twelve feet of rounded, lime-green Bug drew his quick frown.

"Have you ever driven with a tree strapped to your roof?"

"Not exactly. No," she finally admitted, leaving him to assume that her husband had been behind the wheel. He also figured that the guy had transported prior trees on something considerably larger than what she drove now. Or they'd had it delivered, given what she'd said about the sort of family she'd just shed.

"Then you need to know that the weight affects the way a car handles. Especially if it's windy, and we have a wind advisory for the weekend. Make sure they net it for you. It'll be easier to manage that way. And take a blanket to protect your roof. Have someone help you secure it, too. You want it tied tight so it doesn't slip."

She hadn't thought about the weather. Rain at least part of the day was a given. It was the Northwest. She didn't like wind, though. It made inclement weather that much more miserable.

"Did you *promise* Tyler you'd have it up tomorrow?"

"It was the only thing I could think of to take his mind off having to change schools."

"Did it work?"

Her little boy hadn't budged from the window. He hadn't even taken off his jacket.

"Not as well as your lights did."

The admission would have made him smile, had he not just caught the hint of defeat in her voice. Or maybe what he heard was simply fatigue.

"Tell you what." Totally sabotaging his plan to stay away, he did a quick reschedule. "I'll only be a half an hour away from you tomorrow. What time will you be at the lot?"

"About the same time you said you have to be in Ta-coma."

"I'm just picking up parts from a machinist. I'll leave earlier and be at the lot about twelve-thirty." It would take an hour to pick up the tree, an hour plus to get back. That left him plenty of time to drop off the parts at the boat-works, get home, shower, change and get to yet another client's holiday party. At least this time he didn't have to pick up a date. He didn't have one.

"You don't have to do that, Erik. You've done enough," she insisted, obviously referring to the lights. "We'll man-age."

"We? You mean you and Tyler?"

"We're the only we here."

"Look." He was really getting tired of the I-don't-want-to-be-obligated-to-you tone that had slipped into her voice, but he had neither the time nor the inclination to argue with her. "You've said you want this Christmas to be good for your son. I assume that means you don't want him to have memories of his mom having a meltdown because his tree fell off the car and the car behind her hit it and turned it into kindling. Or because the thing weighs a ton and she can't get it into the house. Or into the tree stand, for that matter. You have a tree stand, don't you?"

"Of course I do. And I don't have meltdowns," she re-plied. "Especially in front of my son."

"No. You probably don't," he conceded, not at all sure whom he was annoyed with. Her. Or himself. "You just suck it up and try to deal with everything on your own. It's fine if you want to be independent, Rory. I'm sure you have your reasons for being that way. But this isn't about creating an obligation, or you owing me if I help you. It's about Tyler. All I want to do is help with the tree. For him. Okay?"

Silence.

About the time he thought she might simply hang up, she said, "Okay. For Tyler."

"Good. I'll be at the lot tomorrow with my truck." With a glance at his watch, he winced. "Right now I've got to get to this payroll. I'll call you when I'm on my way."

He should probably apologize.

The thought crossed Erik's mind every time he noticed the wary way Rory watched him the next afternoon. He just wasn't sure exactly what he should apologize for. He hadn't said a word to her that wasn't absolutely true. And she'd definitely needed the help.

The rain came in fits and starts. The weather was cold, the temperature dropping, the wind blowing, and the tree Tyler had selected after carefully checking out the small forest under the huge canvas tent was not only the eight-foot maximum she'd given him, but rather wide. Even tied up to make it more manageable and tarped to keep it dry, with the heavy wind gusts, getting it to her place on the rounded roof of her car would have presented a definite challenge. So would the task of her and Tyler unloading the thing and carrying it into the store to get it into its heavy iron stand, a task that involved sawing off a couple of lower limbs and trimming the thick trunk to make it fit before tightening the screws into place.

Mother and son wrestling it into the house on their own would have presented its own set of frustrations. Especially since carrying it into the house through the store—which had been easier than putting it in the stand in the garage and carrying it through the mudroom—involved hoisting the stand end of the eighty-plus pounds of bushy branches, trunk and iron to his shoulder while she brought up the rear with the top end and Tyler ran ahead of them to open the door.

He said nothing about any of that, though. It wasn't necessary. The process proceeded far easier with his truck and his help, and that was all he'd wanted: to make something a little easier for her and her son—and to offset his guilt over having pushed her about the store to the point where she'd given up sleep.

"Where do you want it?" he asked.

"In the corner by the fireplace. On the towel so the stand doesn't stain the carpet."

"Can I help?" called Tyler.

"Just stay back for a minute, sport. I've got it." He told Rory, "You can let go."

Behind him, Rory stepped back as the weight lifted from her shoulder. With a quiet whoosh of branches and the thud of heavy metal on towel-covered broadloom, the stand hit the floor and the tree popped upright.

The whole room suddenly smelled like a pine forest.

Beside her, her little boy grinned. "It's really big, huh?"

Not just big. For the space, it was huge, definitely larger than what they would have wound up with had Erik not been with them. Fuller, anyway.

She'd realized within minutes of arriving at the tree lot that what she'd promised her son would have been a night-mare to manage on her own. On their own, they also would have wound up with something more in the five-foot range.

"Thank you," she said to Erik's back.

He turned, pushing his windblown hair back from his forehead.

"No problem. This is the fourth tree I've hauled this month." He wanted her to know that what he'd done wasn't a big deal. Not to him, anyway. Certainly nothing she needed to feel obligated to him for. "The one at work, a neighbor's and one of Pax's cousins'."

"Do you have a tree?" Tyler wanted to know.

"I don't usually put one up."

"How come?"

"Because I'm not home in the evenings much this time of year and I go to my folks' for Christmas."

Her little boy's brow pinched. Before he could voice whatever had him looking so concerned, Erik motioned to the single green bin sitting near the fireplace.

"You want the rest of those?" he asked her, referring to the others still stacked in the store.

She started to tell him she could bring them in herself. Thinking it wiser to accept his help than risk resurrecting the tension that had ended their phone call last night, she said, "Please," and hurried after him to help.

Tyler wanted to help, too, so she had him carry in their new two-foot-high, red-velvet-clad Santa with its price tag still attached while they brought in the bins filled with the lights and ornaments she'd need for the tree.

The only other thing she needed, other than for the heavy caution between them to ease, was to start a fire in the fireplace to take the deepening chill off the room. While Erik went back for the last bin, she crumpled newspaper under some of the kindling she and Tyler had found by a cord of split logs in the lean-to behind the garage.

Erik had barely walked back in when he shot a narrowed glance at the parka she still wore. Tyler hadn't taken his off yet, either.

"Did you turn off the heat?" he asked, hoping she hadn't gone that far in her efforts to conserve.

"I turn it down when we leave, but it's always colder when the wind blows. It just hasn't been this windy. Or this cold. It's freezing out there."

The house had always been drafty. As his grandmother had done on especially cold days, Rory had closed her heavy drapes over the big expanses of glass to insulate from the chill. With the wind that blew the rain against the windows stirring the fabric, he figured he should probably check the weather stripping.

Just not now. For now, all he'd do was make sure she had enough firewood and get out of there.

"There's plenty," she assured him when he said he'd bring some in. "Tyler and I carried a load into the mudroom this morning."

"Can we decorate now?" Tyler asked. "If you don't have a tree," he said to the man checking his watch, "you can help decorate ours. Mom said she'd show me her magic ornaments. You want to see 'em?"

"Magic ornaments?"

"Uh-huh. They're in here." With his arms still wrapped around the Santa, he bumped his little boot against a bin she'd brought in that morning. "She showed me a heart and a bell. I get to see the rest when we put them on the tree."

He looked eager and hopeful and was still running on a sugar high from the hot cider and big candy cane he'd been given at the tree lot.

"We've kept Erik long enough, honey." She hated to burst his little bubble, but with Erik frowning at the time, it seemed apparent he was anxious to go. She felt anxious for him to go now, too. Every time she met his glance she had the uncomfortable feeling he was wondering how she would ever manage there on her own. Or thinking about how much longer the project had taken than he'd probably planned. "He said he had to leave by four," she reminded him. "Remember?"

"But he doesn't have his own tree, Mom. We're s'posed to share."

They were indeed, which left Rory at a loss for a reasonable rebuttal. She didn't doubt her child's disappointment. Yet that disappointment didn't seem to be only for himself. It was as much for the man she sincerely doubted needed anything from them at all.

"I suppose I could stay a little longer," he said to Tyler,

touched by the child's concern, ignoring her. "How much do you think we can do in thirty minutes?"

"We have to put the lights on before we can do anything," she pointed out to them both. Thirty minutes would barely get them going.

"Then I guess that's where we start." He looked to where she suddenly stared back at him. "Unless you hadn't planned on doing this right now."

He had accomplished his mission: delivering the tree. It hadn't occurred to him that he'd even want to stick around and decorate the thing. Especially with Rory stuck somewhere between grateful for his help, not wanting to have needed it and uncomfortable with his presence. Her little boy's excitement with the process, though, and his innocent desire to share that experience with him held far more appeal just then than heading home to get ready for yet another evening of schmoozing and champagne. Even if he didn't leave for another half hour, he'd barely be late. He just wouldn't stop by the boatworks.

Both males expectantly waited for her reply. That Erik seemed to want to stay caught her totally off guard. Considering how he'd practically bolted out the back door the last time he'd been there and how annoyed he'd sounded with her on the phone yesterday, she'd thought for sure that he'd be on his way as soon as he'd delivered Tyler's tree.

Not about to deliberately disappoint her son, and determined to not upset the precarious equilibrium between her and her mentor, she lifted both hands in surrender. "If we're doing lights, we need a chair," was all she had to say before Tyler started pulling off his coat and Erik started heading toward the dining room table.

On his way, he pulled his cell phone from the front pocket of his jeans.

"I need to tell Pax I won't be in today," he told her, punching numbers. They didn't need the parts until Monday, but his partner would be expecting him. "Just give me a minute."

Taking her animated little boy's jacket, she slipped off her own and headed into the mudroom to hang them up. As she passed Erik, she heard his easy "Hey, buddy" before he relayed his message, told him where he was and added that he'd see him "later at the party."

Marveling at the man's social life, and unsettled to find herself wondering yet again about the woman he'd taken out last week, she walked back into the kitchen moments later to see him still on the phone.

"No, I'm not 'seriously preoccupied,'" he good-naturedly defended. "I've just been getting a tree into a stand. What are you talking about?

"You're kidding," he muttered, and headed for the dining room window.

The moment he pulled back the closed drape, she heard a soft ticking against the glass. Little was visible in the gray light beyond. Blowing rain obscured the view.

His brow furrowed. "Turn on the TV, will you?" he asked her.

"What's going on?"

"Everything's closing down," was all he said before she grabbed the TV's remote.

With Erik joining her on her left, still listening to Pax, and Tyler smashed against her right leg, hugging Santa, the three of them watched the churning weather map on the screen while the authoritative voice of the weatherman warned everyone to stay off the roads. The ticker on the bottom of the screen listed temperatures in various degrees of freezing in Seattle and surrounding areas as the voice went on about predicted accumulations of freezing rain or sleet. Another voice took over as the picture switched to a weather cam with a blurry image of a multicar pileup on I-5.

A viewer video showed the sleet-shrouded image of a ferry rocking at its landing.

"What about the Narrows Bridge?" she heard Erik ask Pax.

The furrows went deeper. "Got it. Sure. You, too, man," he concluded, and ended his call.

Sensing the adults' concern, Tyler pressed closer as he looked up. "Is this a bad thing, Mommy?"

It wasn't good. "It's okay, honey. The weather is just causing a few problems," she explained even as more personal complications dawned.

"Nothing you need to worry about, sport."

Peering around his mom, Tyler looked to the man smiling over at him.

"All you need to worry about is finding a place to put that big guy." Erik nodded to the Santa that was nearly half Tyler's size. "Then we can start on the lights."

His concerns appeased, Tyler plopped his Santa on the floor beside him. Suggesting he put the decoration somewhere a little more out of the way, Erik turned to Rory.

"Pax said they're closing the airport, bridges, ferries and freeways. The roads are all iced." His partner had gone over to their client office. The one by Cornelia's. Now he was stuck there.

Given that the bridge he himself needed to take to get back was closed and that the ferry would be down, he seemed to be stuck where he was, too.

He could usually roll with anything. He just wasn't quite sure how the woman who'd just drawn a deep breath and turned away felt about having him there for a little longer then she'd expected. She didn't say a word as she knelt beside one of the bins and popped off the lid to reveal dozens of neatly wrapped strings of lights.

"We're having soup and sandwiches for dinner," she finally said.

Lifting out two strings, she stood up, turned to face him. "Since it seems you're here for the night, you can stay in my room."

His left eyebrow arched.

Mirroring his expression, determined to prove she could hold her ground with him, Rory added, "I'll sleep with Tyler."

Chapter Seven

Rory left the door to Tyler's room halfway open and paused at the top of the stairs. Her little boy had fallen asleep within seconds of his head hitting the pillow. No surprise considering how exciting the day had been for him and how hard he'd fought to stay awake after supper to finish the tree.

From downstairs, the television's barely audible volume told her Erik had switched from *How the Grinch Stole Christmas* to the news.

She hated the ambivalence creeping back as the low tones mingled with the beat of the sleet on the roof, the muffled sound of it pinging against the upstairs windows. The thought of riding out the ice storm in a still unfamiliar house would have had her anxious on a number of levels, had it not been for Erik.

She felt safe with him there. Physically, anyway. And there wasn't a single part of her being that didn't want exactly what he had just helped her provide for Tyler: an afternoon and evening of moments he might always remember as special.

That, in a nutshell, was her problem. His presence provided as much comfort as it did disquiet. Tyler had turned to her every time he'd had a question about where an ornament should go, but it had been Erik's assistance or advice he'd sought if he couldn't get it on a branch, and his approval he'd wanted with nearly every accomplishment.

She didn't want him being so drawn to the man.

She didn't want to be so drawn to him herself.

Wishing she still had her chatty little boy as a buffer, she headed down the steps, stopping when she reached the foyer.

Erik stood with his back to her, his heavy charcoal pullover stretched across his broad shoulders, his hands casually tucked into the front pockets of his jeans as he faced the talking head on the television. The size of the blaze in the fireplace indicated that he'd added another log. Strewn around him were empty bins and ornament boxes. In front of the sofa, the large, square coffee table held a red candle in a beribboned glass hurricane and the last of the crystal icicles waiting to be hung on the brightly lit tree.

As if sensing her presence, Erik turned toward her. She immediately turned her attention to cleaning up the mess.

"Is he asleep?" he asked.

"We barely got through brushing his teeth."

"I'm surprised he made it that far." Seeing what she was doing, and how deliberately she avoided his eyes, he picked up a bin that had held the faux evergreen boughs now draped over the stone fireplace mantel, set it in the entry and put another on the coffee table for her to fill with what she collected.

"Thanks," she said quietly.

"Sure," he replied, and finally found himself faced with what he'd managed to avoid the past few hours.

It had felt strange decorating her tree. Partly because he'd never helped decorate one with a small child buzzing around his knees, partly because the feel of the room with her understated touches in it was completely different from what it had been years ago. What he'd felt most, though, was the need to get past her guardedness with him. That caution still tempered her smiles, and made him more conscious of little things like how her animation had died when she'd opened a bin to see a Christmas stocking embroidered with *Dad.* Her wariness with him wasn't anything overt. It wasn't even anything someone else might notice. Probably something even he wouldn't notice, if he hadn't known he was responsible for it.

He never should have kissed her. The thought had crossed his mind a thousand times in the past few days, usually right behind the memory of how she'd practically melted in his arms. He'd yet to forget the sweet taste of her, the perfect way she'd fit his body. It was as if the feel of her had burned itself into his brain, leaving nerves taut, distracting him even now.

He shouldn't have gotten so annoyed with her on the phone last night, either, though he was pretty sure that same sort of frustration had been at least partially to blame. But the storm wasn't letting up anytime soon, the thickening ice made escape next to impossible and he didn't want this evening to be any more difficult than it needed to be. Short of apologizing to her, which he had the feeling would only make matters worse, especially for the kiss part, he'd do his best to put her at ease with him some other way.

She'd just reached up to hang a fallen ornament high on the tree. As it had every other time she'd reached that high, the motion exposed a thin strip of pale skin between the hem of her short white turtleneck, shorter green vest and the dark denims hugging her sweetly rounded backside.

"So," he said, forcing his focus to something he wanted

to know, anyway. "What's with the 'magic' ornaments?" He nodded toward the empty shoe box on the end table. "You told Tyler all those you took out of that box appeared out of nowhere."

The tiny crystal ice skates, the little Eiffel Tower stamped *Paris, Texas,* the miniature pink-and-white cupcake—all the ornaments in her "magic" collection looked much like the other decorations sparkling on the tree. Yet she'd even handled them differently, more carefully, he supposed.

"That's because they did," she replied, lowering her arms to pack up more empty boxes. "It didn't matter where my parents and I were, every Christmas morning I'd open the door and there would be a package with a gold box tied with a red bow. Inside would be an ornament that had something to do with where we were staying. Or something I was into at the time."

"Did your parents leave them there?"

"They had no idea who sent them. There was never a return address."

"So that's why you call them magic," he concluded.

"It was more than that." Conscious of him watching her, she packed the boxes into the bin he'd set on the coffee table. "It was what I felt when one of those little packages appeared. That's what made them magic. At that moment, no matter what town we were in, with Mom and Dad mine for the day and that gift in my hands, I had the feeling that everything was right in my little world." That was the feeling she wanted Tyler to know. He deserved that. Every child did. "I wound up with fourteen of them."

"It sounds like you moved around a lot."

"We did. Mom and Dad still do." Their mailing address was their agent's. "They're musicians."

His brow furrowed. "So what's wrong with that?"

The question brought a quick frown of her own. "I didn't say anything was wrong with it."

"I didn't mean you. You said the other day that Curt's parents had a problem with you being his secretary instead of a lawyer. That things got worse when they found out your 'people,'" he repeated, making air quotes, "weren't the right pedigree. What's wrong with being a musician?"

Her instinctive defense eased with his mystified tone. Marginally.

Apparently he had her a little edgier than she'd realized.

"There wouldn't have been anything wrong with it if they'd played the violin or French horn in a symphony, but Dad plays bass guitar and Mom is a singer in a rock band. That was not the image Audrey wanted their friends to have of their son's wife." She closed the lid on the now full bin and moved to fill another. "On the rare occasion mention of my family came up, she said they were in the music industry and changed the subject."

Unlike nearly everything else she'd exposed about herself the last time Erik had been there, she'd forgotten she'd even alluded to her parents. She'd be the first to admit that their decidedly bohemian lifestyle hadn't provided the most stable environment, but it wasn't as if they'd tattooed her forehead and named her Moonbeam or Thistleweed. They were good people who just happened to be creative, extroverted free spirits who'd never figured out which of them possessed the recessive "conventional" gene each accused the other of passing on to her. They were her mom and dad. She loved them. She didn't understand them, but she loved them.

"Are they any good?"

"They're very good."

"Where do they play?"

"Sometimes they get a gig doing backup for tours," she told him, grateful for the ease of his questions as they worked. Relieved, too, that he wasn't letting her dwell on her former in-laws' biases.

Trying to appear as comfortable with their present situation as he did, she looked around for anything she'd missed. "Mostly they're on a circuit where they play small venues for a few weeks at a time."

"That had to make for an interesting childhood," he muttered, and handed her the stack of boxes from the sofa.

"I suppose it was." After adding what he'd given her to the last bin, she snapped on its lid. "I just never knew where we'd be next, or how long we would be there." *Fluid,* her mom liked to call their lives.

"But a little gold box showed up everywhere you went." The container now filled, Erik picked it up to stack with the others. "Just trying to get the rest of the story," he explained, and waited for her to move so he could carry it to the door.

She stepped aside, pretty sure he would have moved her himself if she hadn't.

With him carrying away the last bin, she scooped up a few of the crystal icicles and snowflakes still on the coffee table, started hanging them on the tree. "They showed up every year until I stopped traveling with my parents," she told him. "Mom and Dad had been playing in Seattle and I didn't want to move around anymore. I'd just turned eighteen, so I stayed here when they left for their next engagement. That was the first Christmas a package didn't show up. We finally figured out it was their booking agent's wife who'd been sending them. Apparently, he represented a few other artists who traveled with their kids and she did it for all of them."

"Nice lady." Erik came up beside her, pulled one of the icicles from her hand. "So where will your parents be this Christmas?"

"Colorado. They're booked through New Year's."

He glanced at her profile as she lifted another bit of crystal above her head to hang on a high branch. She wouldn't have family around, he realized. Not liking that thought, not questioning why, he took the icicle from her and hung it below the white angel on top. As he did, he caught the clean scent of something herbal mingling with pine. Her shampoo.

The fragrance was subtle. Its effect on him was not.

Intent on ignoring both, he took one of the snowflakes. "So what will you and Tyler do? Go to a friend's house? Have friends over?"

He was just making conversation. Rory felt certain of that. And the question seemed casual enough. It was his nearness, and the answer, that gave her pause.

"We'll just stay here. My girlfriends from Tyler's school will both be out of town."

"What about other friends?"

"Except for work and Tyler's school, I wasn't involved in much the past year. Most of the other people I socialized with were in Curt's circle. Members of the firm and their spouses," she explained. "I don't belong in that group anymore."

For a moment Erik said nothing. Beyond them, the low voice of the weatherman droned on, the fire snapped and crackled. He could let it go, move on to something less personal. His mention before of the man she'd married— his relatives, anyway—had dented the calm facade she'd worn for her son the past few hours. But her guard with him had finally slipped, and his curiosity tugged hard.

"You said Curt had a different area of practice," he reminded her, "but was he in the same firm as his father and brother?"

With a faint frown, she handed him the last two ornaments she held and turned to pick up more for herself.

"Different firms. Both firms belong to the same country club, though. It's where the guys play racquetball and squash and wine and dine their clients. For the most part," she qualified, moving back to the tree. "Curt liked us to entertain at home." He'd seemed proud of her skills as a hostess, too, she thought, only to banish the memory before others could take hold. The moment she'd seen his stocking a while ago, the old doubts had rushed back, adding a different sort of disquiet to an already challenging day.

"You lived in the same circles as his parents?"

"It's not like we saw them all the time," she replied, hearing the frown in his voice. "But the wives of some of the partners in Curt's firm were on the same committees as Audrey and her friends. The ones who don't work outside their homes, anyway. Symphony. Heart Ball. That sort of thing."

"And you?"

"I was on them, too. For a while." She'd done her best to help Curt's career any way she could. They'd been a team that way, a more intimate extension of the partnership they'd developed when he'd been her boss and she his secretary. Or so she'd thought. "Our personal friends were more into getting together for dinners, or taking the kids out for lunch after T-ball."

"What about them?"

"What do you mean?"

"Why don't you ask them over? I bet Tyler'd be up for it."

She was sure he would. It just wasn't that simple. And what Erik was asking was really quite sweet. Surprising. Unexpected. But sweet—if such a word could be applied to the six feet plus of disturbing male quietly messing with her peace of mind.

It seemed he didn't want her and her son spending Christmas Day alone.

"That's the group I don't belong to anymore." The other one, the country club set, she'd never really had. "I was part of a couple with Curt," she explained, wondering how long it had taken the man beside her to think of himself as an *I* rather than a *we* after his wife had gone. "After he died, the guys didn't have their colleague and I was a reminder to the wives of how their lives would change without their husbands. Or how their lives might not even be what they'd thought they were," she concluded, only to find herself in the one place she hadn't wanted to go.

The place where so many questions begged for answers that would never come because the only person who could provide them was no longer there.

She wasn't at all sure how their conversation had taken such a swerve.

"What part wasn't what you thought it was?"

Her eyes met his, old pain quickly masked as she glanced away.

"All of it." She gave a brave little laugh, tried to smile. "So any advice you have about how to move beyond something I can't do a thing about would be greatly appreciated. Something more immediate than a five-year plan would be nice."

Perspective. That was what she needed. Since she couldn't imagine how she'd ever have it where her marriage had been concerned, the least she could do was maintain some about the too-attractive man who'd kissed her senseless four days ago and now acted as if nothing had happened at all—which she would be eternally grateful for, if she could somehow forget it herself. He was her mentor. Granted, he was her business mentor, but maybe the more she reminded herself of his place in her life, the less she'd be affected by things like the swift concern lowering his brow. Since his place in her life was to provide advice, she might as well take advantage of his counsel.

"Do you want to be a little more specific?" he asked.

Pretty certain the tensions of the day had just caught up with her, she dropped her glance to the slender ornament between her fingers. What she wanted had nothing to do with the store. But Erik did have a certain amount of experience in this particular area. He'd lost someone who'd once been important to him, too.

"I overheard some things at Curt's funeral that I can't seem to forget. About our marriage," she explained, her voice quietly matter-of-fact. "Since he's not here for me to ask about them, I think what I really want is to know how long it will take before the answers don't matter so much."

Erik watched her blink at the ornament, her eyebrows knitted as she stared down at what she held.

She'd never told him what had happened to her husband. Neither Phil nor Cornelia had mentioned it, either. And he hadn't wanted to ask. It had seemed to him that the less he knew about her, the easier it would be to keep her pigeonholed as a project, a duty. Something with a start and end date that required nothing of him in between but a little business advice and elbow grease.

It would have helped enormously if her little boy had been a brat.

It would have helped even more had she not been trying so hard to move on.

"What happened to your husband, Rory?"

Her focus remained on the light reflecting off the crystal. "He was on his way home from work. It was late and a drunk ran a red light." The twin slashes between her eyebrows deepened. "He was dead at the scene."

The unnatural calm in her voice belied how totally her world had shattered at that moment. That same stillness held her there, motionless except for the movement of her finger along the spiral facets.

"And what had you heard that you couldn't ask him about?"

She barely blinked. "That he'd married me to spite his parents.

"It was after Curt's funeral," she added quietly. "At the reception." His parents had wanted the reception after the service at the club. She hadn't cared where it had been held, had been fine with going in whichever direction she'd been pointed. Other than Tyler, she hadn't cared about anything at all.

"I was in the restroom when some other women came in. They didn't know I was there because I overheard one of them ask how long Curt and I had been married. One of Audrey's friends told her, then said I was nothing like the women he'd usually gone out with. Refined women, she'd called them. I heard someone else say that everyone knew he'd married me just to spite his parents. Apparently, not long after Audrey heard we were dating, she started setting him up with women she thought more appropriate. The more polite consensus was that he'd married me to get her off his back."

That was the only clear memory she had of that entire day. So much of it had been a fog of hugs, sympathetic murmurings and just wanting to find the friends watching Tyler and get her son out of there.

She absently hooked the icicle she held onto the nearest branch. "He'd never told me his mother was doing that. But it could certainly explain why he'd wanted to elope." She'd thought at the time that his idea to run off to Lake Tahoe had sounded wonderfully romantic. But at barely twenty-one, what had she known?

"I'd been happy. I'd thought he was, too." Her hand fell, her voice along with it. "He'd always put in long hours. But that last year he'd put in even more. He'd been trying to make partner," she said, though she had no idea why the detail even mattered now. "After hearing those women, I couldn't help wondering if he was really away so much because of work. Or because he just didn't want to be there with me and I'd been too naive to realize it."

Her throat felt oddly tight. It had been well over a year since she'd verbalized that fear. She'd found out later that some of their friends had heard the rumors that day, too. Audrey, grieving herself, and in an apparent effort to save face for both of them, had even called her the next day to apologize for her friends' "lack of sensitivity at such a time." She had not, however, denied their conclusions.

Rory swallowed. Hard.

Feeling nearly as bewildered and betrayed as she had that awful afternoon, she pushed her fingers through her hair, trying desperately to force a smile. "I think now would be a really good time for you to give me the estimate I'm looking for. Six more months? A year? Please just don't say 'never.'"

For long seconds, Erik said nothing. He remained an arm's length away, his thoughts about the women's thoughtlessness anything but charitable, and fought the instinct to pull her into his arms.

He'd had closure when his marriage had fallen apart. He'd had answers to his questions. After he'd divorced, there had been no doubt in his mind that his marriage had been irreparably broken. The way this woman's had ended, she was left with questions that could never be answered.

Not by the man she'd married.

He seriously questioned Curt having had any ulterior motive when he'd married her. There was far too much about her to be attracted to, too much to truly care about.

Since the guy wasn't around to tell her what all those things were, he'd just have to enlighten her himself.

"Come here."

Taking her by the hand, he led her toward the wing chair by the sofa, muting the television on the way, and nudged her to the cushion. With his side to the fire, he hitched at the knees of his jeans and sat down on the heavy hassock in front of her.

Resting his forearms on his thighs, he clasped his hands loosely between them. "You want my take on this?"

Her arms crossed protectively at her waist, she murmured a soft, "Please."

"For starters," he began, being as objective as possible, "it's far more logical to conclude that he married you not to spite his parents, but *in* spite of them. You're beautiful, smart and easy to be with. For the most part," he qualified when she blinked at him in disbelief. "You can be pretty unreasonable at times," he pointed out, mostly so he wouldn't have to consider how unwillingly drawn he was to her himself. "But, trust me, he was attracted to you. He had to be." Especially if she'd showed up at the office looking the way she had the other night in that suit and heels.

"As for what those big mouths in the bathroom said about you being different," he continued, "you probably were. If he'd been going out with society types or old money or whatever his mother considered 'refined,' you'd have been a breath of fresh air."

A few years out from leaving the mobile nest of her fairly unconventional parents, there probably hadn't been an ounce of pretension about her. Even now, the polish he suspected she'd acquired in her husband's circles seemed as understated as her quiet sensuality. There was something about her that defied definition. It was almost as if her desire for permanence had forced her from her parents' artistic, nomadic lifestyle to seek stability in the urbane and conservative and she'd yet to find where she was comfortable in between. What truly impressed him, though, was the strength that pushed her past what many would see as totally daunting obstacles, along with a seemingly innate ability to nurture, to ease and to make a man feel as if every word he uttered mattered.

The way she made him feel just then.

"He might not have even realized how constrained he

felt until you came along." Thinking of the emotionally vacant relationships he personally limited himself to, he cleared his throat, glanced from the quiet way she watched him. "You went to work as his secretary. Right?"

Looking a little doubtful about his assessment, she gave a small nod. "He'd been there four years."

"So even before you came along, his career choices made it pretty clear he had a mind of his own. It sounds like he was willing to follow the family profession, but on his own terms. When he did meet you, I doubt he gave a second's thought to what his mom and dad would think. By the time he realized he wanted you in his life, their opinion might have mattered to him, but not as much as you did."

He knew for a fact that the physical pull between a man and a woman tended to lead the way where the sexes were concerned. If Curt had been half the man Erik suspected he was, he'd have had as hard a time as he was at that moment keeping his hands to himself. On the parental objection front, he couldn't imagine his own folks finding any fault with her at all.

"As for eloping," he continued, not at all sure where that last thought had come from, "he probably knew his parents wouldn't be willing participants, so it just made sense to avoid the problem. Most guys I know prefer to duck all the big wedding plans, anyway. Unless that's what his fiancée really wants," he qualified, because he'd given in on that one himself.

A bit of red glitter clung to one knee of her jeans. With the tip of her index finger, she gave it a nudge. "I didn't care about anything big, Erik. I just wanted to marry him."

He had no idea why that didn't surprise him. What did was how a while ago, he'd wanted details. Now, he did not.

"A little more insider info here," he offered, despite a stab of what felt suspiciously like envy. "Men aren't that complicated. If Curt was like most of us, if he was working longer hours, he was just doing what he needed to do to get ahead in his field and provide the kind of life he wanted for his family. It's what a guy does," he said simply. "Our egos tend to be tied to what we do for a living. But our work is also how we take care of the people we care about."

As if he'd just touched on something familiar, her glance lifted, then promptly fell.

She'd forgotten how often Curt had told her that he wouldn't be putting in those hours forever. That soon he'd be a partner and they could afford a bigger house, better cars, the kinds of vacations he wanted them to take. So many times he'd told her he was doing what he was doing for them.

She'd loved him for that. But she also remembered telling him she couldn't imagine living in a house larger than the one they had. She'd been fine—more than fine—with everything they'd already possessed.

"I think he needed bigger and better more than I did."

"That's entirely possible." Erik watched her nudge again at the bit of sparkle, the rest of her fingers curled into her palm. "A lot of people measure their success by their acquisitions. Especially if the people around them do the same thing." He wouldn't be in business himself if there weren't people who wanted to own the exclusive sailing sloops he loved to build. "That doesn't mean he wasn't thinking of you. And Tyler. And don't forget, he also cared enough about what you had together to work through the…ah… baby problem you two had," he decided to call it, "and adopt that great little guy upstairs."

What she had recalled moments ago had put a microscopic tear in the doubts that had caused her to question nearly every memory. Erik's conclusions had just ripped that hole wide.

She had no secrets from this man, she realized. There was nothing of any import about her he didn't know and, in some inexplicable way, seem to understand. Because of that he had just reminded her of a time when she had known without a doubt that her husband loved her. Curt had been so worried about losing her, of her thinking less of him because he couldn't give her the child they'd both wanted so much. Yet the struggles, disappointments and finally the joy of Tyler had only brought them closer.

So many details of her married life had faded in the past months. So much had been lost or skewed by second-guessing and uncertainties. But that much she remembered with crystal clarity, and while the memory was a bittersweet reminder of what she had lost, it also felt mercifully…healing.

"As for the rest of it," he said quietly, "if you were happy and if he seemed happy with you and Tyler, that's all that matters." Without thinking, he reached over, traced his finger over hers. "If you'd stop looking for ways to explain what you heard, I think you'd probably know that."

The tip of his finger moved over her knuckles, his touch gentle, reassuring. His strong hand looked huge next to hers, and she wanted badly to absorb his certainty as he uncurled her fingers and rested his palm on the back of her hand.

"Do you think you can do that?" he asked.

Watching his fingers curve around hers, she gave another little nod.

"That's a start, then," he murmured.

He had no idea how far beyond a start he'd led her.

At that moment, with Erik doing nothing but holding her hand, she couldn't help but think of how Curt would have really liked this man. She could have hugged him herself for defending Curt the way he had—had she not already been wishing he would hold her.

He tipped up her chin, curved his hand to the side of her face. "Are you okay?" he asked.

Her heart gave an odd little bump. "Sure."

"You're a really lousy liar."

She had no idea what he saw in her expression. She just knew her throat felt suspiciously tight as his dark eyes narrowed on hers.

"You'll be all right, Rory. I don't know how long it will take for you," he admitted, surprising empathy in the deep tones of his voice. "It was a couple of years before I realized I was having a good time again. But you'll get better before you even realize it's happening."

Her head unconsciously moved toward his palm. The heat of his hand felt good against her cheek, warm, comforting. Grounding. At that moment, she just didn't know if it was that anchoring touch or his confident assurance that she needed most. She felt relieved by that contact. It was as if he was letting her know she wasn't as alone as she so often felt. She craved that security as much as she did his disarming gentleness when his thumb brushed the curve of her jaw and edged to the corner of her mouth.

His eyes followed the slow movement, his carved features going taut as he carried that mesmerizing motion to her bottom lip.

Her breath caught. When she felt his thumb give a little tug, her heart bumped hard against her ribs.

An instant later, his jaw tightened and his hand fell.

At his abrupt withdrawal, disappointment shot through her. Swift and unsettling. She wouldn't have pulled away, wouldn't have done a thing to stop him had he moved closer. Knowing that, embarrassingly certain he did, too, Rory rose before he could and reached for an empty mug on the end table.

"Sorry," she murmured. "I said I wouldn't do that again. Dump on you like that, I mean."

When she turned back, Erik had pushed himself to his feet.

Beyond his broad shoulders, a log broke in the fireplace, embers spraying upward. The tick of ice blowing hard against the window grew more audible with another gust of wind.

The storm added yet another layer of unease.

"I asked," he reminded her.

"That's true." Hoping to shake how he unsettled her, she tried for a smile. "So it's your fault."

She was talking about his uncanny ability to uncork her most private concerns. From the way his glance dropped to her mouth, he seemed to be thinking more of the seductive pull snaking across the six feet of tension separating them.

Or maybe it was just her own tension she felt.

"Just part of the service."

He'd only been doing his job.

The reminder had her ducking her head as she turned away. It didn't matter that she'd wanted his kiss, or how badly she'd wanted him to hold her. It didn't even matter that she didn't trust what she'd felt when she'd been in his arms before, that almost desperate need to hide in his strength.

He'd offered her his help, a little comfort and his experience. What he wasn't offering was a refuge, and she had no business thinking of him as one.

"If you don't mind, I think I'll just say good-night now," she murmured. "You're welcome to stay down here and watch TV if you want. My bedroom is the one—"

"I know where your bedroom is, Rory."

Of course he did.

"The sheets are clean and I put clean towels in the master bathroom." Her bathroom wasn't very big, but he already knew that, too. "I set out a new toothbrush for you."

"I'll figure it out," he assured her. "Is there anything you want me to do down here?"

"Just bank the fire."

The rest could wait until morning.

The telltale muscle in his jaw jerked. "Consider it banked. I'll take care of that," he said, taking the mug from her. "You go on up. I'll catch the news for a while and turn off the lights."

He obviously felt the need for a little space, too.

More than willing to give it to him, she started for the stairs.

The silence behind her and the faint ticking of ice against glass had her turning right back.

"Is the roof up there okay? It can handle the weight of the ice, can't it?"

"The roof should be fine."

She lifted her chin, turned back again.

Another step and she turned right back. "Is there anything I can get you before I go up?"

He'd barely met her eyes again before he shook his head and turned away himself. "I don't need a thing," he assured her. "Just go to bed. I'll see you in the morning."

Chapter Eight

For Rory, sleep rarely came easily. When it did, it was usually fitful, an often futile exercise where the loneliness she could sometimes mask with activity during the day reared its ugly head at night to haunt her. But she must have been asleep. Something had just wakened her, a distant, cracking sound followed by an odd, heavy silence.

With Tyler's back tucked against her, she blinked into the dark. Realizing that it shouldn't be that dark since his night-light should have been on, she reached for her robe at the foot of the twin bed.

She had no idea what time it had been when she'd heard Erik come up the stairs and close the door at the end of the hall. She'd lain there listening to the sound of water in the bathroom pipes and the heavy creak of floorboards as he'd moved around her room. When silence seemed to indicate that he'd gone to bed, she'd attempted to block further thought in that direction by listening to her son's deep, even breathing and the wind gusting like muffled cannon blasts against his bedroom wall beside her.

The ice pelting the window had no longer sounded as sharp, as if the buildup had muffled it. The only thing that had allowed her to not feel as anxious as she might have about the fury outside had been thinking about the man down the hall being so near.

Now she heard nothing at all.

There was no clock in Tyler's room. Quietly, so as not to wake her sleeping child, she pulled on her robe and found her way to the door.

The moment she opened it, she realized the electricity had gone out. The night-light in Tyler's bathroom across the hall wasn't on. Neither was the one in the outlet down by her room. The hall was as black as pitch.

She kept a flashlight in her nightstand, another in a drawer in the kitchen. Without questioning why she didn't head for her room, she edged toward the stairs, her hand sliding along the wall to guide her to the handrail.

"Rory?"

Her hand flattened over the jolt behind her breastbone. "Erik," she whispered, turning toward his hushed voice. "Where are you?"

"By your bedroom door. Where are you?"

"By the stairs," she whispered. "What was that noise?"

"It sounded like a tree went down. My guess is that it took out a power line." Across twenty feet of dark came the soft, metallic rasp of a zipper. "Do you have a flashlight up here?"

It seemed he'd just zipped up his jeans. Thinking he could well be standing there shirtless, she murmured, "The nightstand on the left. In the drawer."

She heard him move inside, and his mild oath when he bumped into something, the end of the bed, probably. Moments later, shadows bounced around the room and a flash of bright light arched low into the hall. Following that blue-white beam, he walked up to her, his undershirt and sweater in his free hand, and handed her the light.

She kept the beam angled down, the pool of it at his feet. Still, there was more than enough illumination to define every superbly sculpted muscle of his chest.

Deliberately, she moved her glance to the heavy sports watch on his wrist. "Do you know what time it is?" she asked.

"Almost seven."

It would be getting light in less than an hour.

He dropped the sweater. In two quick motions he shoved his beautifully muscled arms into his long-sleeved undershirt.

"When you did the walk-through with the building inspector, did he say anything about the generator? It should only have taken seconds for it to take over."

The generator? "He said it was set to come on for a few minutes once a week," she told him, scrambling to remember as she watched him pull his shirt over his head. "To make sure it'll be available when I really need it," she added.

Erik's dark head popped out, rearranging his already sleep-mussed hair. His jaw was shadowed, hard and angular in the dim light. "Has it been working?"

"I don't know." The gray metal generator on the slab at the back of the building hadn't been on her priority list. It hadn't been on her list at all. Until now. "I think he said it's set for either Tuesday or Wednesday mornings. We haven't been here then."

He swiped the sweater from where it had landed near her beam-lit, glittery-red toenails. Rising, his glance skimmed the length of her pale robe, only to jerk away before he met her eyes.

She'd barely realized he looked nearly as tense as he

had when she'd left him last night before he dragged the sweater over his head and tugged it down. "I'll check the transfer switch. Then I'll get a fire going.

"I just need this." He took the flashlight from her. "Give me a minute and you'll have enough light to do whatever you need to do up here. The hall light won't work, but the bathroom lights will. Did he explain how the standby works?"

A transfer switch sounded familiar. The guy who'd inspected the building a couple of weeks ago had pointed it out. It was in one of the electrical panel boxes in the basement.

"I think so. I don't remember everything he told me," she admitted. "We looked at a lot around here that day." There'd also been Tyler to calm. He hadn't liked the huge, shadowy space. "There was a lot to take in."

Something shifted in Erik's expression. She knew he'd been aware of how overwhelmed she'd been by Cornelia's intervention, and by how suddenly she'd found herself in a place she'd known nothing about at all. It stood to reason there were a few things she might have missed, or had forgotten. As it was, she could have managed on her own to start a fire to keep Tyler warm. She just had no idea what to do about the generator—which meant, right now, she couldn't fix this particular problem without him.

She didn't doubt that he knew that, too, as he followed the beam of light down the stairs, pulled on the heavy boots he'd left at the bottom and disappeared into the dark.

Feeling at a distinct disadvantage where he was concerned, and hating it, she turned in the dark herself, working her way first to Tyler's bathroom, then back to his room. She'd just started to put on the clothes she'd left on his play table last night when she heard his bedclothes rustle.

"Mom? I'm a-scared."

"It's okay, honey. I'm right here. The power went out," she explained, her voice soft, "but it'll be back on in a minute." Leaving her robe on, she found her way to him, hugged his warm little body to hers. "You don't need to be afraid." Forcing a smile into her voice, she murmured, "You know what?"

His response was the negative shake of his head against her neck.

"I have a big surprise for you."

"Is the tree all done?"

"It is. But that's not the surprise."

She felt him pull back. "Is he here?"

He. Erik.

The man's presence was not at all the news she'd hoped would get his morning off to a better start.

"He's downstairs," she told him, and felt certain he'd have scooted off the bed that very moment had he been able to see where he was going.

She'd thought to tell him her surprise was the big adventure the day might be, since making an adventure of uncertainties, for the most part, had taken his mind off his fears and insecurities before. Since Erik had unknowingly just accomplished that for her, she told him they'd just wait right where they were while his idol turned the lights back on.

Instead of electric lights, however, it was the beam of the flashlight that illuminated the hall outside the open door.

The beam swung inward, causing Tyler to bury his head in her chest at the momentary brightness and her to block the sudden flash with her hand.

"Sorry," Erik muttered. He aimed the beam at the rumpled bedding on the trundle. "It's not the switch. I'll have to wait until it's light out to see what the problem is."

The circle of light bouncing off the cerulean sheets

filled the room with shades of pale blue. Along the far wall, he watched Rory cuddling her son on the higher bed, her hair tousled, her hand slowly soothing the child's flannel-covered back as Tyler turned to smile at him.

It hit him then, as they sat huddled in the semi-dark, that all they really had was each other. He'd realized that on some level last night when he'd prodded her about where they'd spend Christmas. But seeing them now, realizing how much she'd lost and how vulnerable she could easily feel being that alone here, drove that reality home.

The troubling protectiveness he felt for her slid back into place. That same protectiveness had been there last night, protecting her from him.

He'd had no business touching her last night. All he'd wanted when he'd met them at the tree lot yesterday was to make sure she could give her little boy the Christmas she wanted for him.

All he'd wanted last night was her.

There hadn't been a trace of defense in her pretty face when he'd touched her. Nothing that even remotely suggested she would have stopped him if he'd pulled her to him. He'd known when he'd left there a few days ago that distance was his best defense against complications with her. Especially since the not-so-subtle needs she aroused in him simply by her presence had a definite tendency to sabotage objectivity where she was concerned.

Having sabotaged the distance angle himself simply by showing up, it seemed like some perverted form of justice that distance was going to be deprived him for a while.

"Do you have another flashlight up here?" Objectivity now appeared to be his only defense. And objectively, she truly needed far more help from him than a little tutoring with the store. "Something stronger than this?"

"The only other I have is just like that one. It's in the kitchen in the phone desk drawer."

"You need something brighter. I'll get one of the camp lamps from the store and bring it back for you to use up here."

She didn't know she had camp lamps. But then, she hadn't finished her inventory, either.

"We'll wait," she told him, then watched him leave them, literally, in the dark.

There was something he wasn't telling her. She would have bet her silk long underwear on that, had she not needed to wear it under her favorite gray fleece sweats to keep warm.

She couldn't believe how quickly the house had cooled. She turned the thermostat down every night, but without the furnace running at all, the temperature inside had dropped ten degrees within the hour.

She'd compensated by bundling Tyler in long johns, fleece pants, heavy socks, slippers, an undershirt, thermal shirt and sweatshirt and parking him under a blanket in front of the blaze Erik had built in the fireplace.

The only layer Erik had added was his jacket when he'd gone out a few minutes ago. He'd already left it in the mudroom when the thud of his heavy-treaded work boots announced his return.

"This is the last of the wood you brought in yesterday. I'll get more from the shed in a while."

The drapes were still closed, but the edges of the room were no longer dark. The fire had grown to throw flickering light into the room. The camp light that now occupied the dining table illuminated from that direction much like a table lamp.

Tyler smiled up at him.

"Can we turn on the tree?" he wanted to know.

He hadn't been talking to her. "We don't have electricity yet," she reminded him anyway. "Why don't you read

Frosty?" With the suggestion, she handed him his new favorite picture book. "And I'll get you something to eat."

Concern suddenly swept his little face. Dropping the book, he shoved off the blanket and headed for the wall of drape-covered windows.

"Is there a problem with the furnace, too?" she asked Erik, wondering what her little boy was up to. Wondering, too, if a problem with the furnace was what the larger male wasn't sharing. "It's oil. Not electric. Shouldn't it be working?"

Tyler pulled back the living room drapes. Dawn lightened the window, but the coating of frost and ice on the glass made it impossible to make out anything beyond it.

The logs landed with quiet thuds at the far end of the hearth. "The furnace is oil, but the fan and pump are electric. You need power to pump the oil and push out the hot air."

Great, she thought. "Oh," she said.

Tyler let go of the drape. The heavy fabric still swung slightly as he ran to the dining room window next to it and pulled back the drape there.

"How come I can't see it?" he asked.

"See what, honey?"

"The snowman. He has lights."

"Hey, Tyler. I heard your mom say she'd get your breakfast. How about we get that out of the way before we tackle anything else?"

At the obvious change of subject, Rory's glance darted to Erik. It was met with the quick shake of his head and the pinch of his brow.

He moved to her side, his voice low. "I don't think you'll want him to see it yet. Give me time to fix it first. I haven't been all the way around the building, but some of those gusts last night were pretty strong. You might want to take a look from the store porch.

"So," he continued, brushing off his hands as he walked over to the child smiling up at him. "Why don't you show me what kind of cereal we're having?"

Totally distracted by his friend's attention, Tyler dutifully led the way to the pantry while Rory grabbed a flashlight and headed for the door into the store. On the way, she could hear Erik asking questions about flakes versus puffs and Tyler answering like an expert before she closed the inner door and hurried by flashlight beam to the outer one.

She'd barely opened the store's front door and screen and crossed her arms against the freezing air when she froze herself.

The world outside had been transformed into a wonderland as disheartening as it was beautiful. In the pale twilight, the stubbles of her lawn appeared to be a blanket of clear marbles. Across the ice-glazed street, every bough on every tall pine, every branch of every winter-bare tree, every leaf on every bush had been encased in a robe of ice.

In between, the ice-coated electric line sagged heavily from pole to pole—except for where it dangled loose a few feet from the tangle of branches of an oak tree now uprooted from her yard and lying across the road, blocking it completely.

Near the entrance to her driveway, half of the maple tree that would shade it in summer lay squarely in it.

Clouds filtered the cold sunrise, but the sky to the east was lightening enough to add hints of color to the gray when she carefully edged her way over the icy boards to the end of the porch and looked toward the meadow. It was there that she saw the snowman that now rested in parts not far from the still upright and remarkably unbroken apple tree. The white chicken-wire, light-encrusted balls had separated when they'd blown over and were now frozen in place with boughs that had flown in from the grove of pines beyond.

Erik had suspected that seeing the dismembered decoration would have upset her little boy. He was right. And though what she saw distressed her, too—especially when she thought of what had to be an identical mess of toppled debris on the other side of the building—she wouldn't let herself think about how she was going to clean it all up right now. Mother Nature froze it, and she'd thaw it, too. She'd worry then about taking care of the scattered and broken boughs, branches and trees. Right now she couldn't let herself think about anything beyond going back inside, making sure the guys were fed and figuring out how to make coffee without any power.

The rest of it was just too daunting.

"Thank you," she said softly on her way past Erik the moment she walked back in.

He stood at the island, Tyler a few feet away at the silverware drawer. "No problem." He searched her face quickly, looking to see how she was taking what she had seen.

Not sure what to make of the deceptive calm she diligently maintained around her child, he turned with two boxes in his hands. "Cereal?"

"Sure." Doing her best to ignore the knot of anxiety in her stomach, she reached for bowls and bananas. "What kind are you having, Ty?"

"Both," her son announced.

"We're mixing 'em," Erik explained.

The camp light now stood on the kitchen counter. In that relative brightness, Tyler's eyes fairly danced.

The dark slash of Erik's eyebrow arched. "Is that a problem?"

For a moment she thought the suggestion must have been Erik's, until she considered that Tyler could have come up with the idea and Erik had decided to let him think the notion a good one. Looking between the two of them, she decided it could go either way. And either way, as protective as Erik had been of her son's feelings moments ago, and sensing that what that mountain of muscle really needed was to be outside and moving, she couldn't think of a thing to say but, "Of course not."

Being deprived of his usual five-mile morning run did nothing to help Erik escape the restiveness nagging like a toothache as he headed into the early morning light. The bracing air felt good, though. He didn't even mind that the ground felt like a skating rink beneath his boots. His balance on it was as sure as on a yawing sailboat—managing that shift and roll was second nature to him.

Where he was out of his element was figuring out how to stay objective about the woman inside when he'd been kept awake half the night by her scent on her sheets and thoughts of her tantalizing little body playing havoc with his own.

When he had first agreed to help her, he hadn't considered how much her education would require beyond a business plan and inventory. But the scope of his responsibility had finally hit him. It had taken both of his grandparents to maintain their store and their home. For her to make it here, she'd need to be as self-reliant as they had been.

What he also hadn't considered until a while ago was how much more difficult her tasks might be because part of her focus would almost always be on her child.

Ten minutes and another trip to the basement later, she had power—which was one less thing he needed to be concerned about before he headed back upstairs to see her by the light switch in the dining room.

"You fixed it." Relief lit her guarded smile as she pushed the toggle. "I heard the refrigerator come on. And the furnace."

From where he'd stopped in the entryway, he watched her glance up at the still dark fixture above the long table.

"That light is off circuit right now," he told her. "The only overhead light you have up here is in the kitchen. Besides the bathroom lights upstairs, you have one live outlet in each bedroom. All the appliances up here have power. So does the water heater in the basement, but the washer and dryer don't."

The minor inconveniences barely fazed her. "What was wrong with the generator?"

"The fuel line valve from the propane tank had been left in the off position. It could have been turned when the servicing company filled it, or by the inspector when he checked it out. Either way," he said, conscious of her concentration, "it would be a good idea for you to check it the next time it's filled. I'll show you later how to thaw the valve in case it ever freezes in place again. Right now there are a few things I want to show you in the basement."

"I wanna go to the basement," Tyler announced.

Rory looked to where he had just jumped to his feet. "I thought you didn't like the basement."

With a small shrug, he walked up to Erik.

"It's okay," was all Tyler said, but it was infinitely more obvious than Erik's faint smile that it was only okay because of the big guy.

With more immediate concerns to deal with, she knew she couldn't afford to worry about that growing attachment now. His new hero had the vaguely impatient look of a man on a mission as he led them down the steep stairs and across the concrete floor.

Because Tyler wanted to see what he was talking about, he scooped him up, catching his small hand to keep him from touching anything, and proceeded to describe how the transfer of the power between the generator and the grid took place and how this system had a double-pole, double-throw transfer switch gear as a safety feature because it was the best way to prevent shock or electrocution.

Her son looked fascinated by what the big man holding him so easily was saying about currents, shutoffs and sensors. And while she grasped the basics of what she needed to know, much of the detail escaped her just then. She had no problem, however, recognizing when something could be dangerous. As the day wore on, she even found herself wondering if there was any double sort of safety feature a woman could use to protect herself from the effects of a man who had the disturbing ability to draw her to him even as he pushed her away.

"I just want to know how to use a regular saw. Okay? The one you used to trim the trunk on the Christmas tree would work fine."

"It would work on the smaller branches," Erik agreed, the icy breeze carrying away the fog of his breath, "but not for those you need to cut to get something this size moved. If you're serious about this, a chain saw is faster and a lot less work."

Concern clearly battled her determination.

"If I'm using that, I won't be able to hear Tyler if he needs me. And I can't have him right with me, because I don't want him anywhere near that thing."

"I'll show you how to use the handsaw." He didn't hesitate to offer the assurance, aware himself of the child on the porch, breaking ice off the fir boughs she'd collected for a wreath. "But you should know how to use this, too. We'll be where you can keep an eye on him."

He watched Rory look from the wicked-looking chain saw blade to the long tangle of ice-coated limbs that had split away from the maple on the far side of the drive. A slash of exposed, raw wood on the heavy trunk mirrored the ragged tear on the thick branch where it had fallen from the tree's side.

He'd already cut up the branch that had fallen atop it with the now-silent saw he'd borrowed from her neighbor. He'd heard the saw's droning buzz when he'd come outside a couple of hours ago to fix Frosty and put a little physical distance between himself and his charge. Being near her in the confines of the house had left him too edgy, too restless. Outdoors, he at least had the buffer of space.

His glance slid from her burgundy fleece headband and jacket to the hem of her jeans. Since she'd kept herself occupied away from him for the better part of the morning, he suspected she'd been after a little distance, too.

Apparently having reassessed her options, and with her immediate concern addressed, she anchored the toe of her black boot in the loop of the saw's handle. "So," she gamely began, "I start it by putting my foot here?" she asked. "And pulling on this?"

Catching her arm as she reached for the starter pull, he turned her in the churned-up gravel to face him. "You start by putting on these."

He tugged off his heavy leather gloves, then slipped the clear safety goggles Ed Shumway also loaned him from around his neck.

Teaching her how to use a saw hadn't been on the agenda he'd outlined for himself that morning, but she'd wanted to know how to use one to clear the property after it thawed. Since he didn't much care for the thought of her outside sawing and hauling limbs by herself, he'd already planned to have the mess cleared for her. This wasn't the only storm she'd likely ever encounter, though. And he wouldn't be around once she was on her financial feet. If she was going to be self-sufficient, it was his job to give her the tools she'd need to make that happen.

Reaching toward her, he looped the goggles' wide elastic strap around the back of her head. Not giving her time to take off her gloves to adjust the bright orange band, he did it himself and settled the clear skilike goggles in place.

"Keep in mind that the barter system still works for a few things around here, too," he informed her, tucking back a strand of the dark hair he'd dislodged from the fleece covering her ears. "Someone should be willing to take care of all these trees for you in exchange for a load or two they can sell or use for firewood."

Far too conscious of the softness of her skin, the silk of her hair, he deliberately dropped his hand.

Pulling his gloves from where he'd tucked them under his arm, he jerked them back on and nodded to the saw. "Now you can start it."

Rory braced herself. Not so much for what she was about to do, but because everything about this man had her feeling so off balance.

He'd given her his jacket a while ago. He stood there now in his heavy charcoal pullover and jeans, seeming totally unfazed by the cold and the almost familiar ease with which he'd touched her.

"Hold the blade straighter," he called over the din of the idling motor. With his broad chest pressed to her back, he reached his arms around her, placed his gloved hands over hers and adjusted her angle.

"Ready?" he asked, his breath warm through the soft knit covering her ear.

Conscious of his body enclosing hers, she gave a tense little nod.

She wasn't sure which disconcerted her more, the thirteen pounds of suddenly screaming machine, or the man surrounding her, making sure she didn't hurt herself with it. With the blade engaged, metal teeth spinning, the chain bit ice. A quick spray of what looked like snow and wood chips flew.

"Keep your grip steady." He spoke near her cheek now, his body still at her back as he eased his hands to her shoulders. "You need to keep it from bucking back if you hit a knot. Keep it under control."

Control, she thought. She hadn't felt "in control" in ages.

"Like this?" she called, handles in a death grip, her eyes glued to the blade sinking into the wood.

"Just like that," he called back and, just like that, the weight of the free end of the limb cracked it downward and the blade went through.

A second of disbelief was replaced with a grin as she swung toward him.

"Don't!" His hand shot forward, the side of his face bumping the corner of her goggles an instant before his hand caught hers to hold the saw in place. Bent against her, he'd turned his head to hers, his lips inches from the startled part of her own.

"The brake," he said. With a small movement of his hand, the throttle dropped back to idle. "You need to set it as soon as you finish your cut. It's safer that way."

She realized now why he'd stayed behind her. Had she swung around, she could have caught him with the blade in his thigh.

Taking the idling machine from her, he shut off the motor, set the saw on the ground.

In the sudden silence, she could hear her heart hammering in her ears. Shaken from the start he'd given her, horrified by what she could have done to him, she dropped her glance to the short placket on his pullover as he rose and turned to her.

"Erik, I'm so sorry."

His forehead furrowed as he pulled her hand from her mouth and lifted the orange band at her temples. Removing the goggles, he looped them over the fabric covering his forearm.

"Hey. It's okay." Hating how he'd killed her quick smile, he touched his gloved finger to her high cheekbone. It was there that the goggles would have bumped. "We hadn't gotten to that part." Another second and they would have, he thought, searching her pale features. He just hadn't expected her to get excited about felling a limb. "Next time you'll remember."

He couldn't feel the smoothness of her skin through the thick suede. He could imagine it, though. Just as he could too easily imagine so many other things he knew he shouldn't be thinking about her.

Detachment wasn't an option at the moment. Not with her looking so frightened by what she could have done. "Right?"

Beneath his hand, he felt her faint nod. What he noticed most, though, was how her head turned toward his hand, as if somewhere in her subconscious she craved that unfettered contact, too.

She'd done the same thing last night, right about the time he'd been thinking about reacquainting himself with the feel of her mouth. Heaven knew how tempted he'd been to do just that. But he acknowledged now what he hadn't then. It hadn't just been complications with her he wanted to avoid. He hadn't wanted her thinking of anyone but him when he kissed her. And last night had been far more about easing the doubts that had haunted her for so long than whatever it was that kept him from caring about how easy she was to touch.

Rory watched his glance shift over her face. She had no idea what he was thinking, what it was vying with the concern so evident there, but from the way his eyes narrowed on her cheek, he seemed to be looking for a bruise.

"It didn't hurt," she told him, praying she hadn't caused him one as she unconsciously lifted her hand to his temple.

"I don't see a mark," he murmured. "But that doesn't mean you won't have a bruise later. You should get some ice on it." He gave her an encouraging smile. "There's plenty of it."

She felt far too concerned to smile back. "I don't see one on you, either," she told him, tipping her head to get a better look. "Not yet, anyway."

Erik's smile faded. He couldn't remember the last time a woman had touched him simply to make sure he was okay. There was caring in that touch, a hint of worry, a little gentleness. As complex as it seemed, it was really such a simple thing. Something basic. Yet her unveiled concern pulled hard at something deep inside him. Something he hadn't been sure still existed, and which would have felt decidedly threatening had he had time to consider what it was.

"Mom? Come help me?"

At her son's request, Rory's hand fell. Only now aware of how she'd reached to be sure Erik was all right, and of how they must look standing there checking each other out, her glance darted to where Tyler stood by a stack of pine on the porch.

He wanted help with the wreath.

Taking a step back, she called that she'd be right there.

Erik met her lingering disquiet.

"Stop worrying. You're quick. You'll get the hang of this," he insisted. "We'll give it another try later. In the meantime, you did fine. Really."

"Except for the part where I nearly disabled you," she muttered, half under her breath.

"I had you covered, Rory. You were a long way from anything like that."

A split second was hardly a long way. She'd have

pointed that out had his assessment of her capabilities not just registered. It was like last night, she thought, when he'd talked her through the doubts and turmoil of the past year. It seemed he didn't want her doubting her abilities, or herself, about anything.

He clearly expected her to challenge his last claim. The quick part, probably. She couldn't. Last night he had called her beautiful, smart and stubborn. The stubbornness she would concede. That he thought her beautiful and smart still left her a little stunned. But what mattered to her most was that for him to feel so certain about her meant he might actually believe in her himself.

Until that moment, she hadn't realized how badly she wanted that sort of faith—that trust—from him.

"I'm going to go help Tyler now."

His eyes narrowed on hers. "You're good, then?"

He wanted to know if she believed what he'd said.

I had you covered, Rory.

"I'm good," she said, and with him already turning to his task, she headed for the porch to rescue the boughs and her rosy-cheeked child.

He had her back. He wasn't going to let anything bad happen as long as he was there.

He couldn't begin to know how much that assurance mattered to her.

Chapter Nine

Erik had told her not to worry.

Rory wasn't sure she knew how to do that. The unwelcomed trait had become second nature. Yet what concerned her far more than her lack of skill with gas-fueled equipment was how she found herself wishing Erik's solid presence could be part of the community that encouraged her with its potential.

Ed Shumway, the neighbor who'd loaned Erik the saw, was married to Edie, the loquacious neighbor who'd first welcomed her to the neighborhood. He had come to repay Erik for his assist moving a limb from his garage that morning. Having heard on the news that it would be at least two days before crews could get in to restore power, he'd brought his bigger saw to help him clear the uprooted oak from the road that was their main access to town.

Even for her neighbors who didn't have access to TV news, word traveled fast by cell phone. Crystal Murphy, her laugh infectious and her carrot-red hair clashing wildly with her purple earmuffs, brought her four-year-old son to play with Tyler while her husband, Tony the roofer, joined the men. Her mom was at their house a quarter of a mile away with their two-year-old. They didn't have power but that seemed just fine with them. They had a woodstove and kerosene lamps and Crystal confessed to liking the throwback lifestyle. She turned out to be the candle maker Edie had told Rory about.

Jeremy Ott came for the same reason as Tony and Ed. Talia, his wife, who taught riding lessons at the stables a mile farther up, had braved the cold with her five-year-old twins because Edie had mentioned that Rory had a son their age.

Edie herself showed up with her two children, twelve and six, and a half gallon of milk. With all the children, hot cocoa went fast.

Even with all the activity, Rory found her attention straying to the man who stood just a little taller than the rest.

It was nearing four o'clock when the women stepped out onto the porch to see how much longer the men would be. The kids were warming up in front of the TV, under Edie's preteen's supervision, and it would be dark soon. There were suppers to prepare.

Rory doubted that Erik had taken a real break since lunch. All she'd noticed him stop for was to stretch his back or absently rub his neck before tossing aside another log or attacking another limb on the downed oak.

She was standing by the railing between Crystal and Edie when he made a V of his arm and hitched his shoulder before putting his back into hefting another chunk of tree. He and Tony were hauling cut sections of limbs to the side of the road while the other two men continued decreasing the size of what had blocked it.

Seeing who had Rory's attention, Edie flipped her braid

over her shoulder and tipped her dark blond head toward her. A navy Seattle Seahawks headband warmed her ears.

"He's an attractive man, isn't he?"

"Who?" asked Talia, leaning past Crystal.

"Erik," the older woman replied.

Rory gave a noncommittal shrug. "I suppose." *If you like the tall, dark, unattainable type,* she thought. Suspecting her neighbor was fishing, she glanced to Edie's nearly empty mug. "More coffee?"

"I'm good. Thanks." The loquacious woman with the too-keen radar kept her focus on the men methodically dismantling the tree.

"He and his business partner have done quite well for themselves, you know."

"I'd say they've done extremely well," Crystal emphasized. "Pax—his business partner," she explained helpfully to Rory, "is from here, too. I've heard they're both millionaires."

"I've met Pax. Nice guy," Rory admitted. What she didn't mention was that she already knew that Erik had means—that he even had friends among the very rich and famous.

She had been surrounded by the well-to-do, and those intent on joining their ranks, from the moment she'd married until she'd moved mere weeks ago. The understated way Erik used his wealth and the way he didn't balk at getting his own hands dirty just made her forget that at times.

Edie gave her a curious glance. "Would you mind a personal question? I didn't want to ask when I first met you," she explained. "I mean, I did, but it didn't seem appropriate at the time."

Rory smiled, a little surprised by the request for permission. "Ask what?"

"How long you've been widowed."

"A year and two months."

"That's too bad."

"It really is," Crystal agreed. "I'm sorry, Rory."

"That has to be so hard." Talia placed her gloved hand over her heart. "I don't know what I'd do without Jeremy."

Edie shook her head. "I meant it's too bad it hasn't been longer. I was just thinking how nice it would be if you two hit it off. I'm sorry for your loss, too," she sincerely assured Rory. "But I imagine you need a little more time before you start thinking in that direction."

"I don't know about that," Talia piped in. "My uncle remarried six months after my aunt passed."

"I think men do that because they don't know how to take care of themselves," claimed Edie.

Crystal frowned. "I thought that the men who married fast like that were the ones who'd had good marriages, so they weren't afraid to jump back in."

"If that's true," Talia said, leaping ahead, "then the opposite could explain why Erik hasn't remarried. I've never heard what happened with him and...what was her name?"

"Shauna," the other two women simultaneously supplied.

"Right. She wasn't from here," she explained to Rory. "They met one summer and she moved here after they married, but they left for Seattle after a year or so. My point, though," she claimed, getting to it, "is that maybe his experience has put him off women."

"Oh, I wouldn't say he's off women," Rory admitted. "We've had a couple of meetings where he had to leave because he had a date."

Talia shrugged. "Well, there goes that theory."

"That doesn't mean he's not gun-shy," Crystal supplied supportively.

"True. But Rory's not looking right now," Edie reminded them. "Anyway, I was just thinking it would be nice if Erik would come back. I can't imagine that he ever would," she insisted, certainty in her conclusion. "Not with his business so well established over in Seattle. But he still seems to fit in so perfectly here."

The woman who'd brought up the subject of her potential availability had just as abruptly concluded it. Relieved to have escaped matchmaking efforts, for a while at least, and not sure how she felt having reminded herself of her mentor's social life, Rory found herself silently agreeing with her well-intentioned neighbor.

Erik did seem to fit in. But then, he'd been raised there. Without letting herself wonder why, she'd also wondered if there was ever anything about this place that he missed. Or if his emotional barriers kept him from even noticing.

It hadn't sounded to Rory as if the women knew the other, more personal reasons why he wouldn't be coming back. The dreams he'd buried there. Still, Edie was right. Everything Erik cared about was in Seattle.

And everything she now cared about was here, she thought, and went back to looking a little concerned about him again.

"Why didn't you stop?"

"Because we were almost finished."

"You were out there another two hours, Erik."

"That's close enough to almost. I'll be fine after a hot shower. How did it go with the neighbors?"

The man was hopeless.

"It was nice." You escaped the part where Edie wanted to make us a couple, she thought, but other than that... "Crystal is going to bring me samples of her candles to see if I'd be interested in selling them. And Talia's twins go to the school I enrolled Tyler in. We're going to carpool."

She frowned at the way he cupped his neck as he sat down at the island. He'd said he'd be fine, though. The man had a scar as wide as Tyler's tired smile on the inside of his forearm. It was visible now where he'd pushed up his sleeves. He knew how much discomfort he could handle.

"What are you grinning about, bud?" he asked, tired but smiling himself.

Tyler took a deep breath, gave a decisive nod. "This was the best day ever."

"Wow. That's pretty cool." Forearms resting on either side of his heaped and steaming bowl of stew, he looked over at the little guy who'd mimicked his position. "What made it so good?"

Tyler looked over his shoulder at the white lights softly illuminating the room behind them. The fire in the stone fireplace crackled and glowed.

"My tree. And the ice on everything. And my new friends." He wrinkled his little brow, thinking. "And Mom, 'cause I got cocoa two times. And you."

"Me?" Erik exhaled a little laugh. "What did I do?"

"Well," he began, pondering. "You fixed things. And you made Mom laugh."

Erik's glance cut to where she sat at the end of the island, back to the child between them. "I did?"

"Uh-huh," Tyler insisted, his nod vigorous. "When you dropped your coat on her."

Though Erik looked a little puzzled, Rory knew exactly what Tyler was talking about. The two of them had just gathered boughs for the wreath. She'd been sorting them on the porch, her head bent over their project, when Erik had walked up behind her and asked if she'd take his jacket. With her back to him and him in work mode, she'd no sooner said she'd be glad to when he'd unceremoniously dropped it over her head.

He'd meant it to land on her shoulders. But she'd looked up just then. Heavy and huge on her, she'd practically disappeared under the soft black leather.

She'd already been smiling at what he'd done and gone

still at the unexpectedness of it when he'd lifted the back of the collar and peeked around at her.

"You okay in there?" he'd asked, and the smile in his eyes had turned her smile into something that had sounded very much like a giggle.

She hadn't giggled since she was sixteen.

Erik apparently remembered now, too.

Looking over at Tyler, he gave his little buddy a knowing nod. He remembered the bright sound of that laugh, of hearing a hint of lightness in it he suspected she hadn't felt in a very long time.

"She needs to do that more often," he decided, and after arching his eyebrow at her, suggested Tyler finish his stew before he went after it himself.

Rory glanced away, stabbed a piece of carrot. She wished he wouldn't do that—arch his eyebrow at her that way. Something about the expression seemed teasing, playful and challenging all at once. Except for the challenging part, it also tended to disarm her and she'd been having a hard enough time remembering why she needed to keep her emotional guard in place with him pretty much since he'd strong-armed her into trying Ed's saw. Or maybe the problem had started last night, when she'd unloaded on him. Again. Or yesterday, when he'd sided with Tyler about the size of the tree.

There were reasons. Compelling ones, she was sure. She just couldn't remember them as she gave him her most charming smile and told him there was more stew if he wanted it.

He had seconds, told her it was great, then finished the bit in the pot before she carried his and Tyler's bowls to the sink.

"What Tyler said about it being a good day," he murmured, handing her his milk glass when she came back for it. "It was." He kept his focus on the glass and her hand, his tone thoughtful, as if he was a little surprised by that perception. Or perhaps by the admission.

"Now," he continued, moving past whatever had prompted it, "if you don't mind, I'm going to get that shower. You wouldn't have a spare razor, would you?"

She told him she did. A small package of them was in the drawer below where she'd left the toothbrush on the counter for him last night. She didn't bother telling him they were hot pink.

It did Rory's heart good to know her little boy had had such a good time that day. It did something less definable to it to know Erik had somehow appreciated it, too. Something that fed an unfamiliar bubble of hope that common sense told her was best to ignore. But with Tyler pretty much worn out and in need of a bath, she gave it no further thought. By the time she'd helped him with his bath and his prayers, it was all he could do to keep his eyes open.

Erik seemed to have had the same problem. When she finally came back down the dimly lit stairs, the fire was nearly out and Erik had fallen asleep in front of the television.

He lay stretched out on the sofa in his jeans and pullover, one leg angled with his bare foot on the cushion, the other foot on the floor. With his dark head propped on the curved arm of the sofa, one arm thrown over his eyes, his other hand splayed on his stomach, it looked as if he'd intended to catch something more entertaining than the weather report before turning in for the night.

The volume on the detective series had been muted, though.

They hadn't talked about it, but there had been no question that he would stay again that night. The negligible melt that afternoon had started refreezing the lower the sun had sunk and, last they'd heard, it was taking forever to get anywhere on the roads. Those that were open, anyway.

That was why he'd followed the Otts home in his monster of a truck, because they'd made the drive on balding tires, and dropped off the Shumways since it was dark by then and they'd all walked earlier.

His breathing was deep and even as she picked up the television's remote and turned off the set.

As exhausted as she suspected he was, she didn't want to wake him. She shouldn't stand there thinking about what a beautiful man he was, either. Or how kind and generous he truly seemed to be even when he didn't want her getting too close. There was something terribly intimate about watching him sleep. Something that might almost have felt intrusive had she allowed herself to remain there any longer.

She lifted the soft throw blanket from the arm of the chair, moved back to lift it over him. Smiling a little at his freshly shaved face, she eased the covering over him. When he didn't move, she let out the breath she hadn't even realized she'd been holding and carefully lifted her hand to his head.

Her fingers had just skimmed the barely damp hair he'd combed back from his forehead when she went still. She hadn't been thinking. She'd simply started to do what she always did with Tyler when she tucked him in and brushed back his hair. The gesture was one of simple affection, of taking care.

As oblivious as he remained to her presence, she let her fingers slip over the soft strands, then curled her fingers into her palm as she stepped away and quietly headed for Tyler's room. Since she felt pretty certain Erik would wake up at some point and head for bed himself, she left the tree lights on so he'd be able to see.

It was to that soft light that he awoke a little after midnight, along with a cramp in his neck and an ache in his back that, he realized an hour later, made sleep impossible.

* * *

Rory heard the faint tap on the door, blinked into the shadows. It had been raining for a while now. She'd lain there, listening to the steady sound of it, imagining the drops taking all the ice away, before the new additions to her usual anxieties about what she'd taken on ruined the little exercise. Everything always felt so much more overwhelming alone at night. With Erik there, she'd at least been able to manage the more restful thoughts for a while.

Hearing the tap again, she slipped from the trundle by the night-light she'd moved to the only working outlet in the room and opened the door.

Her glance collided with Erik's solid, shadowed and bare chest. Down the hall, light from her bathroom filtered through her bedroom door, too dim to reveal more than curves and angles and the shadow of his forearm as he gripped his neck.

He stepped back as she stepped out and pulled the door closed behind her.

She hadn't grabbed her robe. Shivering a little, she crossed her arms over the sleep shirt that barely hit her knees. "Are you just now coming up to bed?"

"I came up a while ago. Do you have anything I can rub on my shoulder?"

He still hurt. Pretty badly, she assumed, to have come seeking help. Feeling guilty that he'd hurt himself helping her, feeling worse because his discomfort was bad enough to keep him from sleep when she knew how tired he must be, she headed for her bedroom door and the bathroom right inside.

The light above the vanity cut a swath across the near edge of the queen-size bed that had once occupied her guest room. If the rumpled purple comforter and sheets were any indication, whatever sleep he had managed had been as fitful as hers tended to be. As she turned into the bathroom, she noticed his nearly dry socks, his long-sleeved undershirt and a pair of gray jersey briefs on the towel rack above the heater vent. With the washer and dryer off circuit, he'd had to improvise.

Realizing what he wasn't wearing under his jeans, she quickly opened the medicine cabinet, pulled out a tube and turned to hand it to him.

He'd stopped in the doorway beside her.

The light was infinitely better here. There were no shadows to hide the broad expanse of his beautifully formed chest, the flare of dark hair, the impressive six-pack of his abdomen or the fact that while he'd zipped his pants, he hadn't bothered with the button.

Her glance jerked up. His hand still clasped his shoulder, his fingers kneading the tight muscles there. But it was his cleanly shaven jaw that held her attention. The hard line of it looked tight enough to shatter teeth. The way he arched his back and promptly winced made it evident his shoulder wasn't the only problem.

His frown of discomfort shifted to the pastel tube he took from her.

"What is this?"

"Herbal cream. I bought it when I pulled a hamstring."

"When?"

"It wasn't anything I did here," she assured him, since she had been known to acquire a bump, bruise or strain herself during her move. "It was in a yoga class. It'll help," she insisted, pretty sure he'd had something more industrial strength in mind.

The skepticism carving deep lines in his face remained as he held up the tube and backed into the bedroom to let her pass. A gravelly edge of fatigue roughened his voice. "I appreciate this. Sorry to wake you."

She didn't bother telling him that he hadn't. Or that she

was actually grateful for the reprieve from her sleeplessness. All that concerned her now was that he was in pain.

"Where do you need that?"

He'd moved to the foot of her bed, away from the narrow shaft of light spilling across the bedding at the corner. Her bare feet soundless on the carpet, she stopped three feet away.

"By my right shoulder blade."

He wouldn't be able to reach there. Not very well, anyway, as stiff as he appeared to be.

"Do you want me to do it?"

He didn't look as if he thought that a very good idea. "I'll manage."

"You're sure?"

"Yeah. I've got it," he insisted, only to wince again the instant he moved his hand in that direction.

Not allowing herself to overthink the situation, she took back the tube. Twisting off the cap, she squeezed a hefty dab of the white cream onto her fingertips and handed the tube back to him.

"You have no business calling me stubborn, you know that?" With him filling the space in front of her, she added, "Turn around," and after a second's hesitation on his part found herself faced with his broad and sculpted back.

In the filtered light, the view of him half naked was no less unnerving, but at least he couldn't see how hard she swallowed before she reached up and spread the cream between his shoulder blade and the long indentation of his spine. His skin felt as smooth and hard as granite when her fingers slipped upward.

Traces of rosemary and mint mingled with the scents of soap, shampoo and warm, disturbing male.

Silence didn't seem like a good idea.

"Why is it that when I came literally a split second from wounding you, you said I wasn't even close? You actually did hurt yourself," she pointed out, rubbing the cream over a knot the size of an egg, "and your 'almost' is two hours."

He lowered his head, gave a small groan with the movement.

"It had to do with circumstances."

She was about to tell him he'd have to do better than that when he sucked in a breath.

She went still. "Did I push too hard?" she asked instead.

His breath leaked out, the tightness in his back audible in his voice. "In a good way."

She'd smoothed her fingers alongside the wide curve of his shoulder blade, the long muscle there as unyielding as the bone beside it. Repeating the motion, keeping the same pressure, she felt his broad back rise as he drew another deep breath, then slowly released it.

What she was doing felt good to him. So she did it again, slower this time. It felt good to her, too, she realized, easing her motions even more. Though she'd tended to fight his efforts, he had been taking care of her in one form or another since the day they'd met. As little as there seemed to be for her to do for him in return, as little as he seemed to want from her beyond what centered on their professional relationship, the least she could do was take care of him now.

"What about the other side? Is it sore?"

"Not as bad."

Meaning it hurt there, too.

Reaching around him, she held out her hand. "I need more cream."

"You don't have to do this," he told her, but even as he spoke, he uncapped the tube and squeezed the analgesic onto her fingers.

"You hurt yourself helping me," she pointed out. "So, yeah, I do." As tall as he was, her elbows were even with her eyes as she raised her arms to work on the other side.

He seemed to realize how far she had to reach.

The bed was right there. "So it's guilt motivating you," he concluded, and sank to the nearest corner. He straddled it, his legs planted wide.

She sat down a little behind him. With one leg tucked under her, the other dangling over the foot of the mattress, she rested her hands on his shoulders to knead the knots with her thumbs.

"Must be," she conceded as he lowered his head again. "Especially since I know this isn't how you'd planned to spend your weekend."

She'd thought before that there were reasons she needed to keep her guard in place with this man. She just hadn't bothered recalling them at the time. With the feel of his big body relaxing beneath her hands, her palms tingling as much from the feel of him as from friction and herbs, it seemed wise to recall those points now.

Reminding herself of the subtle but definite distance he'd put between them last night helped her remember why that need was there. Recalling her comment to the girls about his dates helped, too. There were other reasons, she knew. Even more compelling ones. But for the moment, the last one served her purpose perfectly.

"I'm sorry you missed your party."

"Everybody missed it."

That would be true, she thought, now working her fingers up the cords at the back of his neck. "I'm sure your date was disappointed."

For a moment Erik said nothing. Her fingers were making slow little circles at the base of his skull, reversing their motion to follow the rigid cords to where they met the equally taut muscles in his shoulders.

"I didn't have a date," he finally muttered.

She kept moving down, past the sore spot on the right,

but before he could wish she'd stayed there, she'd continued lower, working her magic along the sides of his spine.

What she was doing felt like pure paradise. She had wonderful hands. Soft. Surprisingly strong. Yet incredibly gentle as she lightened her touch to soothe away the worst of the soreness, then gradually increased the pressure again.

He'd felt a different sort of gentleness in her touch before. He'd thought he'd been dreaming, that he'd only imagined her touching him with even more tenderness—until he'd opened his eyes to see her turning away. The brush of her fingers over his forehead had brought something he couldn't remember ever experiencing from a woman's touch. A feeling of ease, of comfort.

There had been a disturbing contentment to the feeling that didn't coincide at all with the direction his thoughts headed now, but something in him craved that kind of caring. Something undeniable and essential and that should have felt far more threatening than it did with the feel of her small hands unhurriedly working over his back.

The ache running from his neck to the bottom of his ribs had started to ease, the tightness there no longer threatening another spasm. An entirely different sort of tension replaced it as her fingers methodically moved over his skin, massaging toward the base of his spine.

His breath slithered out when she stopped well above the waistband of his jeans. Still, the thought of her dipping her hand lower had every other muscle in his body going taut.

"I thought you might be taking the woman you'd gone out with before," she said into the quiet. "Is she someone you've been with a long time?"

There was nothing deliberately sensual about her touch as she worked her way back up. Nothing provocative in the quiet tones of her voice. Yet the question added a certain strain to his own.

"I haven't been with anyone in a long time, Rory."

Her hands had reached his shoulders. Feeling her go still at the status of his sex life, or maybe the fact that he'd so frankly admitted it, he turned as he spoke, catching her wrist as her hand fell.

"Why the questions?"

Beneath his grip, her pulse jumped.

Rory wasn't sure how to answer. She hadn't expected him to tell her how long it had been since he'd slept with a woman. That hadn't been what she was asking. Or maybe it had been and she just hadn't let herself acknowledge her need to know. The queries had started out simply as a defense against the undeniable emotional pull she felt toward him. She hadn't allowed herself to consider why his being in a relationship with someone should even matter to her. But it had. And he wasn't. And all she could do now was scramble for an explanation that wouldn't betray how very much he already mattered to her. And he did, in ways she was only beginning to comprehend.

"I guess I wanted to know if you were involved with anyone." She lifted her shoulder in a shrug. "Just curious, you know?"

In the pale light, she looked impossibly young to him. Incredibly tempting. Mostly, she looked much as she had last night. Far more vulnerable than she wanted to be, and trying hard for a little bravado.

He saw weariness in her guileless features. He'd heard that same drained quality in her admission. It was almost as if as late as it was, as long as the day had been, she was simply too tired to keep the bravado in place.

"I'm not," he assured her. "I haven't been involved with anyone in years." Involvement implied an attachment he'd avoided for the better part of a decade. A need to be there for someone. A need to let that someone count on him to be there for her. A need to know she'd be there for him.

He'd had absolutely no interest in that sort of commitment. Until now.

"Just curious, huh?"

"A little."

If she'd been trying for nonchalance, she failed miserably.

"You know, Rory," he murmured, self-preservation fighting the need to tug her toward him. "Now would probably be a good time for me to let you get back to bed."

"Probably," she agreed softly. "But I think I'll just go downstairs and read for a while. Seems like a good night to tackle the business plan." She lifted her chin, gave him a tiny smile. "I tried, but I can't sleep."

The simple admission pulled at him, the helplessness in it, the weary frustration of trying to escape what kept a person from rest. What got him, though, was the loneliness she tried to hide with the quick duck of her head.

She'd made no attempt to reclaim her hand, and he couldn't quite make himself let go. Unable to shake the thought of how alone she'd seemed cuddling her son on the boy's bed that morning, realizing how she undoubtedly spent many of her nights, he put self-preservation on hold.

"So what kept you awake? Old worries?" he asked, because he knew how long she'd struggled with them. "Or new ones?"

"Both."

"Today probably didn't help."

He probably hadn't helped. He just wasn't sure how else he could have accomplished what they'd both needed for her to know. Yet while he'd been busy making sure she was aware of everything that needed to be done around the place to keep it up and how to take care of the problems she could expect, the weight of even more responsibility had piled on her shoulders.

"Today was actually a good day." He and Tyler weren't

the only ones who'd thought so. "The worry part is just always there. It's okay during the day when I'm busy, but at night…"

"You can't shut it off," he concluded for her.

"I managed for a few minutes tonight. But then it all came right back."

"What was it about tonight that helped?"

She lifted her glance.

"You," Rory said quietly. Of everything he had done for her in the past two days, everything he'd done in the weeks before, what he had done since yesterday had mattered to her the most. "You being here."

Especially tonight, she thought. Tonight, for a while, anyway, because of him she'd been able to shut everything out and concentrate on nothing but the soothing sounds of the rain still pattering on the roof. Because he was there, because he had her back, because he had everything under control, for the first time in well over a year she'd had a day when she hadn't had to make every decision on her own. She hadn't had to worry about how she would get a tree home for her son, or get one out of her driveway. Or remove the one that had blocked the street. Because of him, they had heat and lights. And for that day, anyway, she hadn't had to handle everything thrown at her alone.

Erik brushed the back of her hand with his thumb, conscious of the small weight of it where he held it on his thigh. The thought that he had somehow given her some measure of relief had just made it that much harder to let her go. Not until she was ready, anyway.

"Do you want to go downstairs?" he asked.

She met his eyes, looked away with a small shake of her head. "Not really."

"Do you want to go back to Tyler's room?"

Another small shake. "Not yet."

"Are you cold?"

"A little."

He knew what she needed even before he asked. He asked anyway. "Could you use a pair of arms?"

That was all he was offering. Just to hold her. This wasn't about wanting her between her sheets. Heaven knew it wasn't about self-protection. It was about giving her a break.

She didn't have to say a word for him to know that his arms were exactly what she needed. But her quiet "Please" was all it took for him to rise and turn out the bathroom light. The night-light now filtering through the doorway cast the room in shadows.

"Come here," he said, and tugged her to her feet.

Leading her to the side of the bed, he pulled the comforter over the sheets and propped both pillows against the headboard. He didn't want her in the bed, just on it.

The distinction seemed just as clear to her as she snagged the wadded throw blanket from the foot of the bed and sat against the far pillow, hugging her arms around her knees when the mattress sank beneath his weight. With his back against his pillow he drew the throw over them both and pulled her knees toward him, his arm low around her back, his hand at the curve of her waist.

"How's this?" he asked, coaxing her head to his shoulder.

He felt her sigh, the long, quiet leak of air leaving her nearly limp against the side of his body.

For a moment, Rory couldn't say a word. She could barely believe she was actually where she had so badly wanted to be. It didn't matter that his jeans felt rough against her bare calf, or that the contrast of his heat and the cool air against the back of her neck made her shiver. She could hear the heavy beat of his heart beneath her ear, could feel it where her hand rested on his hard, bare chest. It didn't even matter that for some strange reason her throat had suddenly gone raw, making her quiet "Good" sound a little tight.

His chin brushed the top of her head as he settled himself more comfortably.

"Good," he echoed, slowly skimming his hand over her upper arm.

She swallowed, then made herself take a deep, even breath. "Erik?" she finally said.

"Yeah?"

"Thank you."

A tired smile entered his voice. "For holding you?" It was hardly a hardship, he thought. She felt wonderful curled up against him. Small, feminine, trusting. The only difficult part was trying not to think of how curvy she truly was with his hand at the dip of her waist, inches from the curve of her hip.

Wanting distraction, he smoothed his hand back up her arm. The herbal scent of her hair teased him, filling his lungs every time he breathed.

"For all of it. But yes." Her tone grew muffled. "For this, too."

He wasn't sure what all she meant. It could have been anything. He just forgot to wonder what might have meant so much to her when he caught the hitch in her voice.

He started to tip up her chin.

She wouldn't let him. Instead, he cupped his hand to the side of her face, brushed it with his thumb and caught the moisture gathered at the corner of her eye.

His heart gave a strange little squeeze. "Hey." *Don't do that,* he thought. He could handle anything but tears. "What's wrong?"

"Nothing. Honest," she insisted, keeping her head right where it was. "Absolutely nothing is wrong." She tried to draw a deep breath, made it halfway before it caught. Swallowing, she tried again. "For the first time in…forever," she said, because that was how it felt, "right now there really isn't a thing wrong."

Which was what had brought the sting behind her eyelids, she realized. Not because of sadness, fear or grief. But because of an amazing, unfamiliar and totally unexpected sense of relief. She knew it wouldn't last long. That it couldn't. It was just for now. While he held her. So just for now, relief was what she felt.

"Then why tears?"

Because of what you let me feel, she thought. "Because I'm tired," was easier to admit to him.

She felt his lips against the top of her head. "Then go to sleep."

"I don't want to."

The slow shake of her head brushed her hair against his chest. Letting his fingers sift through that dark silk, he gave a small chuckle. "Why not?"

"Because I don't want to miss you holding me."

It had to be the hour, the lateness of it, the need for sleep himself. Or maybe it was his need to let her know he'd be there for her in the morning if she'd just let herself rest, but he didn't question what he did as he slipped down, bringing her with him.

His lips grazed the spot on her cheek where they'd literally bumped heads that morning. "You shouldn't say things like that."

Turning her face to him, she whispered, "Why not?"

He'd been about to tell her to go to sleep, that he wasn't going anywhere. But with her sweet breath filling his lungs, the feel of her supple little body playing pure havoc with his intention, he leaned closer.

"Because you'll make me forget why I shouldn't do this," he murmured, and brushed his mouth over hers.

Once.

Again.

"Or this." He carried that gentle caress between her eyebrows, to the space where the twin lines formed when she was worried.

He cupped his hand at the side of her face.

"Or this."

The admission vibrated against her mouth a faint second before he increased the pressure ever so slightly. His lips were firm, cool and far softer than anything that looked so hard had a right to be, but it was the feel of him tipping her head to gain the access he wanted that had her reaching for him herself.

Relief gave way to something infinitely less soothing. It barely occurred to her that this was exactly what she *hadn't* wanted when she found herself opening to him, flowing toward him, kissing him back. She'd known what she would feel if she ever got this close to him again. And she'd been right. She felt everything she had when he'd kissed her before: that deep, awful longing, the yearning to simply sink into his compelling strength, his incredible gentleness, and have him take away the ache in her chest. To relieve the void, the emptiness. Only now with her fingers curling around his biceps and his hand slipping to the small of her back, pulling her closer, the hollowness inside her seemed to be receding, and the emptiness felt more like…need.

When he lifted his head long moments later, his features had gone as dark as his voice. "I think you'd better remind me."

Her own voice came as a thready whisper. "About what?"

He touched the first of the short line of buttons on her nightshirt. His fingers trailed down, found her soft breasts unrestrained beneath thermal cotton.

His lips hovered over hers. "Why we should stop."

Surrounded by his heat, that warmth gathering low in her belly, her voice went thin. "I don't remember."

She didn't know what he saw in her shadowed face when he lifted his head. Whatever it was caused his body to go beautifully taut before his hand slipped over her hip.

"Me, either. But if you do," he warned, the low tones of his voice sounding half serious, half teasing, "stop me."

She was about to tell him that wasn't going to happen, but he lowered his mouth to hers just then and she almost forgot to breathe.

There was no demand in his kiss. Just an invitation to a heady exploration that was deep, deliberate and debilitatingly thorough.

Winding her arms around his neck, she kissed him back just a little more urgently. With him, because of him, she finally felt something other than alone and uncertain, or the need to be strong.

She'd been so frightened by her doubts, so afraid that what she'd thought had been real in her marriage hadn't been at all. If she'd been so wrong about all of it, that meant she couldn't trust her judgment about anything, or anyone, else. But he'd helped her see that she hadn't been wrong about what had mattered most. And more important than anything else he'd taught her, he was teaching her to trust in herself.

She could love him for that alone.

The thought had her clinging a little more tightly, kissing him a little more fiercely. It hurt to know how much of herself she'd let others take away from her. But he was taking that pain away, too, allowing parts of her to come back, allowing feelings she hadn't realized she still possessed to finally surface. For the life of her she had no idea why those thoughts made the back of her eyelids start to burn again. She just knew that at that moment, nothing mattered to her so much as the sense of reprieve she was only now beginning to feel. And the fact that it was he who had finally allowed it.

Erik caught her small moan as she pressed closer. Or maybe the needy little sound had been his own. There wasn't a cell in his body that wasn't aware of how beautifully female she was, and of how badly he wanted her beneath him. To him, she was perfect. Small, supple and infinitely softer than his harder, rougher angles and planes.

He would have just held her if that had been what she'd wanted. It would have about killed him, but he'd have done it. Yet, incredibly, she seemed to hunger for the feel of him as much as he ached for her.

Stretched out beside her, he drew his hand over the nightshirt covering her belly, letting it drift upward, pulling soft cotton away with it. He kissed her slowly, tracing her soft curves, allowing himself the sweet torture of finally knowing the silken feel of her body, the honeyed taste of her skin. He didn't know what to make of the tears he tasted again at the corners of her eyes when he kissed her there, or the almost desperate way she whispered, "No," when he started to pull back to make sure she was all right. Slipping her fingers through his hair, she drew him back to her, meeting him in a kiss that nearly rocked him to his core.

Gritting his teeth against the need she created, he skimmed the bit of silk she wore down her long legs. It landed somewhere beside the bed, along with his jeans.

He'd left his billfold on her nightstand. Some miracle of common sense made him drag himself from her long enough to fumble for the small packet inside. He'd barely rolled their protection over himself when she curled into him, seeking him as he sought her.

The intimacy of gentle exploration had created its own tormenting heat. What they created as they moved together

now, his name a whisper on her lips, had him thinking he'd
never be able to get enough of her before that heat turned
white-hot and he was barely thinking at all.

Chapter Ten

Rory burrowed deeper under her comforter. A delicious lethargy pulled at her, coaxing her back toward sleep. But she heard voices. Male ones. One sweet, the other deep.

Sleep was suddenly the last thing on her mind.

Tyler was awake. Erik was with him. Through the two-inch-wide gap he'd left between the door and the jamb, she could see the light from Tyler's bathroom faintly illuminating the hall. The gap in the curtains next to the bed revealed a thin sliver of gray.

It was daylight. That meant it was somewhere after seven-thirty. She couldn't remember the last time she'd slept that late.

She threw off the covers. Nearly tripping over her night-shirt, she snatched it up and moved to the door. They were just disappearing down the stairs, Tyler in his pj's, Erik in his undershirt and jeans. From the conversation, it sounded as though they were discussing breakfast. Specifically, which one of them got to slice the bananas.

Minutes later, thoughts of how she'd practically fallen apart in Erik's arms adding to the anxiety of wanting to hurry, she'd pulled herself together enough—in the physical sense, anyway—to head into the hall herself.

Slipping a blue corduroy shirt over a cotton turtleneck and yoga pants, she could hear her little guy as she reached the first step.

"Can I help you work today?" he asked. "An' can you help put my train around the tree?"

The low tones of Erik's voice drifted up the stairway. "I think all I'm going to do out there this morning is check the gutters. It's too dangerous for you to help."

"Why?"

"Because it's a long way up there."

"How come you need to check 'em?"

"Because I need to see if the weight of the ice pulled them from their brackets."

"Why?"

She heard a deep, indulgent chuckle. "Because if they're not lined up right, the rain will pour straight off the roof instead of draining to the downspouts and get you and your mom all wet."

Her foot hit the bottom step just as she heard a pondered little "Oh."

Tyler hesitated. "Can we do the train after, then?"

Across the entry, she could see Tyler sitting in front of the lit tree, the blanket she'd covered Erik with last night wrapped around his shoulders. Expectation beamed from his little profile.

Erik sat on the edge of the hearth, his gray undershirt stretched across his broad shoulders as he closed the glass doors on the growing fire.

"I'll have to see how it goes, but I don't know that I'll have time for that, Ty." He picked a stray bit of bark from the stone beside him, tossed it onto the logs in the curved wood basket. "Now that the rain's melted the ice, I need to finish here, then get to my own place."

"You're going home?"

There was no mistaking her son's disappointment at that bit of news. She heard it in his small voice, could practically feel it in him as she watched Erik look up at her an instant before Tyler turned and looked up himself.

Shoving her fingers through her hair, partially undoing what she'd managed to arrange with a few random strokes of a brush, she found it infinitely easier to meet Tyler's sad little face.

"Good morning, sweetie," she murmured, bending to give him a hug. "How did you sleep?"

"Good," came his usual, though decidedly disheartened, reply.

She nudged back his hair, wanting to ease away his sudden seriousness. What Erik had done hadn't been deliberate. There had been nothing but kindness in his voice as he'd explained why he wouldn't be staying. But the painful proof of how her little boy could come to rely on him, could even come to love him, only added to the confusion of wants and uncertainties tearing at her as she kissed the soft, tousled hair at the crown of his head.

"I'll help you with your train later, okay?"

"'Kay," he reluctantly replied.

"So, what's up down here?" she asked him and, as casually as she could, straightened to meet the caution in Erik's smile.

He rose himself, all six feet plus of him, and came to a stop in front of her.

His gray gaze skimmed her face. Slowly assessing. Unapologetically intimate. "The plan so far was to turn on the tree, then build a fire." His eyes held hers. "Then what, Ty?" he asked, since the child hadn't answered his mom.

"Breakfast," came the slightly more enthused reply. "And cartoons?" he added hopefully from below them.

"And coffee?" Erik asked with that disarming arch of his eyebrow.

"Definitely coffee," she agreed.

Grabbing the remote, she punched in the channel she usually only let Tyler watch as a treat. With him on his way to the sofa with his blanket, she headed for the kitchen, Erik's footfalls behind her matching every heavy thud of her heart.

She pulled the carafe from the coffeemaker, turned to see him watching her from beside the sink.

Holding the carafe under the faucet, she turned the water on.

"Why didn't you wake me?" she asked, her hushed voice muffled further by the sound of running water.

"Because I was already awake. When I heard him in the bathroom, I figured he'd come looking for you, so I intercepted him before he could. I thought you might not want him to find us in bed together.

"Besides," he added quietly, "you were out. You barely moved when I pulled my arm from under you."

The reminder of how she'd fallen asleep tucked against his side, their bare limbs tangled, had heat rising in her cheeks.

"I can't believe I didn't hear him." It was so unlike her not to hear her son. "I never sleep that hard." Except with this man beside her, she obviously had.

"Thank you for the rescue," she all but whispered.

He turned off the water for her. With Tyler hidden by the sofa, he lifted his hand, curved his fingers at the side of her neck.

"I'm going to leave in a while," he told her, brushing his thumb over the lobe of her ear. "Pax said everything was okay at the boatworks yesterday, but I have some things I need to do. There's something here I want to check first, though. Is there anything you can think of that you need me to do before I go?"

In the past eight hours, his touch had become as exciting to her as it was calming, as disturbing as it was comforting. He had reawakened her heart and her senses and she'd never felt as confused as she did now, standing there desperately wanting him to pull her to him and hoping he wouldn't.

He'd said he needed to leave, that he had things he needed to do. He'd already talked with Pax, asked about the condition of their properties, their business. She'd heard him tell Tyler that he needed to check on his own place. She knew his entire life was on the other side of the sound. In her need for the temporary escape he'd offered, she'd forgotten that for a few critical hours last night.

"You don't need to check my gutters, Erik."

"Yeah, I do," he said, thinking of her lovely, long limbs and how perfect they'd felt wrapped around him. He'd really prefer that none of them got broken. "It'll save you having to do it yourself."

"I'd have to do it if you weren't here."

The hint of defensiveness in her tone sounded all too familiar.

"But I'm here now," he pointed out, looking a little more closely to see the unease he'd missed in her moments ago.

"You can just tell me what I'm supposed to look for. I'll need to know, anyway."

Caution curled through him. "It's raining out there."

"So I'll wait until it stops."

"That could be June."

He had a point. She just wasn't prepared to concede it. "Is there a particular bracket you noticed?"

There was. The one at the front of the garage that would keep water from pouring over her and Tyler when they came and went from the car. He'd noticed it yesterday and had meant to walk around the garage and the main building to see if any other gaps were visible. But this wasn't about a bracket. It wasn't about a gutter. From the uncertainty underlying her quiet defensiveness, he'd bet his business this wasn't about anything but what had happened between them last night.

Not totally sure what he felt about it himself, not sure what to do about any of it with Tyler wandering over in search of cereal, Erik decided it best to just go do what he'd planned to do anyway.

"I'm going to get the ladder from the basement. I'll be back when the coffee's ready."

It took eight minutes to brew a full pot of coffee. It was another ten before she heard the rattle of the ladder being propped against the wall in the mudroom and the faint squeak of the door to the kitchen when it opened.

Tyler had just handed her his empty bowl and was on his way past the island to go get dressed when she heard him tell Erik he'd be right back.

"Take your time, sport." Ruffling the boy's hair as he passed, Erik looked to where she again stood at the sink.

Still holding the bowl, she watched his easy smile fade to something less definable as he pushed back the navy Merrick & Sullivan ball cap he'd taken from his truck. It looked as if he'd shaken the rain from his cap and swiped what he could from his leather jacket. Beneath it, the charcoal pullover he'd pulled on before he'd gone out was dry, but the darker spots on the thighs of his jeans and the hems looked damp.

"You have two broken brackets," he told her, conscious of Tyler still moving up the stairs. "I'll pick up new ones and be back with them in the morning. I leave for my folks' house in San Diego tomorrow afternoon, so that's the only chance I'll have."

She set the bowl in the sink, picked up the mug she'd taken out for him and poured him his coffee.

Tomorrow was Christmas Eve.

She held the heavy mug out to him.

"You know, Erik," she said as he took it, "you really don't need to come all the way over here to fix those brackets."

The mug settled on the counter beside her.

"I know I don't. And I don't need you telling me that," he insisted, and skimmed her cheek with his knuckles.

The small contact compounded the anxiety knotting behind her breastbone.

Taking a small step back, needing to break his touch as much as the hold he'd gained on her heart, her voice dropped to an agonized whisper. "I can't do this."

Even as his hand fell, his shoulders rose with a slow, deep breath. His hard, handsome features were suddenly impossible to read.

"By 'this' you mean the sex."

"No. Yes." Shaking her head, she shoved her fingers through her hair. "I mean, it's not just that. Making love with you was amazing," she admitted, because it had been. "It's that I can't let myself feel what I'm starting to feel for you." What she already did feel, she thought, and which totally terrified her. "I can't let myself count on you to do things for me. Or for you to be around to talk to. Or for you to be here. If I do, it would be too easy to rely on you even more."

Apparently nothing she'd said explained why she was withdrawing from him. If anything, Erik just looked a little mystified. She figured that was because of what she'd admitted about the sex part. But then, she always had had a problem filtering what she said to him.

His eyes narrowed on hers. "Why not?"

Crossing her arms over the knot in her stomach, her voice dropped another notch. "Because I'm not going to set myself up to lose something I don't even have. It doesn't make sense to do that," she admitted, not sure she was making sense to him. "I can't do that to myself. And I definitely can't do it to my son. It will only hurt Tyler if I let him grow any more attached to you than he already is, Erik. I know people will come and go from his life. People already have, but I've never seen him take to anyone the way he has to you." She'd done a lousy job of protecting herself. That failing would not keep her from protecting her son. "Since the arrangement between us is temporary anyway, it just seems best to back away and keep busi-ness…business."

Her heart hurt. Rubbing the awful ache with her fin-gertips, she watched his jaw tighten as he stepped back.

Erik wasn't at all sure what he felt at that moment. He wasn't even sure what he felt for this woman, beyond an undeniable physical need and a sense of protectiveness he wasn't familiar with at all. All he knew for certain was that they had stepped over a line she clearly had not been prepared to cross.

Recriminations piled up like cars in a train wreck. He'd known all along that it would be a mistake to get involved with her. He'd known from the moment he'd met her that she was dealing with far more than he'd gone through when his marriage had ended. What he didn't understand was how he could have forgotten that his sole goal in agreeing to help her was to have no reason to return to this place once his obligation to Cornelia had been satisfied.

The fact that he hadn't considered any of that last night had his own defenses slamming into place. Having done enough damage already, he wasn't about to complicate their relationship any further. Or let her push him any farther away.

"Just answer one question for me."

"If I can."

"Last night. The tears. Were they because you were thinking of Curt?"

He figured he had to be some sort of masochist for wanting to know if that was what really had been going on with her while they'd been making love. No man wanted to think a woman had another man on her mind while he had her in his arms. Still, for some reason he couldn't begin to explain, he needed to know.

For a moment, Rory said nothing. Partly because the question caught her so off guard. Partly because it was only now that she realized her only thought last night about the man she'd married was how Erik had lessened the void he'd left.

She couldn't begin to explain everything she'd felt last night. Or what she felt now because of his question.

It seemed easiest to just go to the heart of what he really wanted to know.

"The only person in that bed with me was you, Erik."

He heard something a little raw in her quiet reply, something that made her look as if he'd just totally exposed how absorbed she'd been in only him—which was no doubt why she stood there with her arms crossed so protectively and her eyes begging him to go.

He could hear Tyler racing down the stairs.

"We're supposed to meet with Phil after the first of the year." He spoke the reminder quietly, as conscious of the child coming toward them as he was of the definite need for distance. "I don't remember the date, but I'll get it from her. We can figure out our work schedule from there."

"Can we do the train now?"

Tyler had stopped at the end of the island, his expectant glance darting from one adult to the other. He'd pulled on pants and a green thermal shirt and held a red flannel shirt in his fist.

"I have to go now," Erik told the grinning little boy. "But I heard your mom say she'd help you."

His smile fell. "You have to go?"

"Yeah, bud. I do." Unprepared for how the child's disappointment affected him, not sure what to make of the strange hollow in his chest, he tousled his sandy hair one last time, gave him a smile and let himself out through the store.

"Erik! I was just going to call you!"

Erik turned from where he was locking the front door of Merrick & Sullivan's client office. Phil had just emerged from the silver Mercedes parked behind the construction Dumpster in front of the building next door. The tails of her white scarf flew in the breeze as she hurried around to the sidewalk. "Do you have a minute?"

He didn't feel particularly sociable. What he did feel was defensive, edgy and impatient to be on his way. Still, he made himself smile. "Sure," he called back, pocketing his keys. Hunching his shoulders against the chill, he headed to where she'd stopped by Cornelia's building's front door. "What's up?"

"Let's get out of the cold. I'll make us some coffee."

"A minute is really all I have, Phil. I'm leaving to see my folks in a couple of hours."

"Oh. Well, then." Hitching her bag higher on her shoulder, she crossed her arms over her furry white coat. Beneath her matching hat, her eyes smiled through the lenses of her bookish, horn-rimmed glasses. "Rory said you were there when I called the other day. The power being out everywhere had us concerned about her and her son," she explained, "but some neighbors were visiting so I knew we didn't have to worry. We didn't have a chance to really talk, though. Is everything all right with the property?"

Realizing she was checking up on Cornelia's investment

threatened to turn his mood even more restive. "There are a few downed trees and a loose gutter, but no structural damage," he told her, thinking that was about all she'd be interested in. "I heard the power was restored a while ago."

He'd learned that from Ed, who'd done as Erik had asked him to do and called when the area had gone back on the grid. Since he'd told his old friend about Rory's unfamiliarity with the generator when he'd borrowed his saw, Ed hadn't questioned his concern about wanting to make sure there were no other glitches.

Erik hadn't let himself question his concern, either. He'd tried hard to keep thoughts of her and Tyler to a minimum.

"That's good to know. Just one other thing, then, and I'll let you go." She flashed him a smile as she crossed her arms tighter, anxious to get out of the wind. "I take it the two of you were working when the storm hit," she said quickly, making it apparent that Rory hadn't mentioned his insistence about helping with their Christmas tree. "So, how do you think she'll do? Or is it too soon to tell?"

He wanted to say she'd do just fine. She certainly didn't lack for aptitude or the determination to succeed. She even had the incentive of keeping a roof over her son's head pushing her. It would be a challenge doing it on her own, but she'd make a living there. With the connections she was establishing, she'd probably even make a life.

He brushed past the thought that she'd be making that life without him. He had a life of his own right where he was. He had work he loved, a great business, good friends. He had money and the freedom to come and go pretty much as he pleased. His obligation to the woman messing with his carefully constructed status quo ended once they had the business established. Once it was, he could walk away and never go back there again.

"Is there a problem, Erik?"

"No. No," he repeated, waiting for the quick shutdown

of feeling that normally reinforced his last thought. "I'll make it work."

I will. Not *we*.

Phil apparently heard the distinction.

"Isn't she cooperating?"

Not when she was giving him grief about helping her, he thought.

"She just needs a break right now," he decided to say. "With her little boy and the holidays, it just seemed like a good thing to do."

"Was that your idea?"

Initially, it had been. For the business part, anyway.

"The decision was mutual."

"So when do you meet again?"

"Whenever we're scheduled to be here."

"That will be the fifth."

"That soon?"

"At two," she added, and cocked her head. "Do we need to meet before then? We certainly can, if there's ever a problem," she hurried on, having caught his lack of enthusiasm for the meeting. "Part of what we do for our ladies and their mentors is help them work through challenges. Differences of opinion can arise over anything from creative priorities to scheduling—"

"It's nothing like that."

"May I ask what it is?"

It was clearly too late to deny a problem even existed. But all he would admit was, "It's complicated."

"I see." Adjusting the frame of her glasses, she peered at him with interest. "Do you have a solution to the problem?"

He wasn't sure there was one. Not for the two of them. "Not yet."

"Can you work together?"

"Yeah. Sure. There's always email and the telephone." He'd given his word. He'd hold up his end of the deal. For his grandparents. For her. "She wants the business to work. That's what I want, too."

She considered him for a moment, her head tipped thoughtfully, the fine fibers of her white hat fluttering. "You know, Erik, when I gave Rory the address of your grandparents' property, I suggested she look for the possibilities. We knew what she would see when she got there, and that it would be nothing she could have imagined she would want.

"What she'd been looking for was a small home for herself and her son," she confided, "but her needs changed when she lost her job. To see the potential in that property, she had to let go of a mind-set that focused on what she had been looking for and what she now needed. To find the solution to your problem, maybe you should look at the possibilities, too."

She smiled then, gave a little wave of her white-gloved hand. Crystals shimmered on its cuff. "I've kept you long enough," she said. "You have a plane to catch. And I need to get inside before I freeze. Have a safe trip. And merry Christmas."

He thanked her. Added a quick "You, too" and started to turn away.

As he did, his glance caught on the gold plaque engraved with three letters above their doorbell. He'd been curious about it ever since it had gone up last week.

"Hey, Phil," he called, catching her unlocking the door. "What does FGI stand for?"

"It's who we are," she called back. "Fairy Godmothers, Incorporated."

His forehead furrowed. As near as he'd been able to figure out, he'd thought they were in some sort of mortgage business. "Fairy Godmothers? Don't they have something to do with pumpkins?"

"And helping dreams come true." With a charming smile, she disappeared inside.

Mentally shaking his head, he strode toward his truck at the curb in front of his office. He had no idea how anyone over the age of ten could possibly believe in fairy tales, happily ever afters or that other impossibility that Rory had once imagined, Christmas magic. As for dreams, they died by the thousands every day. Reality simply wore them down, if it didn't kill them outright. He knew. He'd spent years in the emotional limbo that remained after his vision of his future had turned to ash. But he'd glimpsed those dreams again, and what Phil had said about possibilities now gave him pause.

She'd said Rory had to let go of a mind-set that focused on what she had been looking for and what she needed now. She'd had to be open-minded enough to see what would be possible living in a place she'd have never considered, rather than writing it off as not what she'd had in mind.

He certainly hadn't considered any sort of personal relationship with her when they'd first met. But one had evolved in spite of him. To see the possibilities in it, he'd need to get past the defenses he'd spent years honing before he could be open to what those possibilities were.

Part of the problem there was that he had no desire to give her a chance to push him any farther away.

The other part would be getting Rory to see past whatever it was holding her back from him to see their potential, too.

Rory had hoped for snow. For Tyler's sake, because that was what he'd said he wanted for Christmas. But Christmas morning had dawned with a gray sky that promised little beyond more rain.

Until a week ago, every other time she'd asked him what he wanted Santa to bring, all he'd wanted was a big tree.

The day after Erik had left, he'd told her he'd changed his mind. Since he already had the tree, what he wanted Santa to bring was Erik.

She'd explained that Erik would be with his parents for Christmas, so Santa wouldn't be able to bring him. Though decidedly let down by that bit of news, he'd decided later that he wanted snow.

All he seemed to want as far as a gift was concerned were things beyond her power to give him.

Without any sort of hint for something that Santa could bring down the chimney, she, being Santa's helper, had left him a mini kick scooter that he could ride between the counters in the store while she worked to get it ready. He'd been excited when he'd come downstairs a couple of hours ago to see it by the tree. He'd been tickled to see that Santa had eaten all but a few crumbs of the cookies they'd left out for him, and awed and delighted by the small tuft of faux-fur trim that appeared to have snagged on one of the fireplace stones when the jolly old guy had departed.

What had truly thrilled him, though, had been discovering the present from Erik among the others from her and her parents beneath the lit and glittering branches. It had been delivered yesterday with a note asking her to please put it under the tree for him to find Christmas morning. Except for the "Thanks" he'd scrawled at the bottom, that was all the note had said.

Tyler had declared the huge pop-up book about sailboats his "very favorite" and gone through every page with her while they sat on the sofa.

It had been only two days since Erik had left her standing in the kitchen feeling as if the world was falling out from under her all over again. Two long nights of missing him more than she'd thought humanly possible. The man was a rock. A truly decent guy. And while she suspected he was fiercely loyal to those he cared about, he held back from needing anyone himself—from needing her, any-way—in the way she now knew she needed him. It wasn't about survival. She could survive on her own. It was about the need to share, and he had worked his way into her life and into her heart as if he was simply meant to be there.

That had only happened with one other man.

Too unsettled to stay still any longer, she left Tyler with his book and cleaned up the bright paper wrappings and ribbons from the carpet.

She had no idea how to repair the damage done to their relationship. He was her mentor. He'd become her confidant. His voice had been one of experience and his advice had been invaluable where other situations were concerned. She just didn't know how to ask what she could possibly do to make things right between them when he was part of the problem, even though she'd picked up the phone a dozen times to try. He had no responsibility to her beyond the agreement he'd made with her benefac-tor, and now even that part of their relationship had been jeopardized.

The two-tone chime of a bell startled her from her pain-ful thoughts. She'd only heard the chime ring twice be-fore: the first morning she'd met Edie, when the woman had stopped by to welcome her to the neighborhood, and two days ago when Talia had brought the twins over to play. Erik had explained that the service bell was used for after-hours deliveries. A few of the locals obviously used it as a doorbell to save themselves from having to walk around back.

Thinking it might be one of the neighbors she and Tyler had delivered Christmas cookies to yesterday, she headed through the store and opened its front door.

No one was there.

Stepping out, the cold breeze tugging at her hair, her

glance caught on a small package on the weathered plank boards.

The little gold box was tied with a red bow.

Now conscious of the dark truck in the parking lot, her heart beating a little too fast, she picked it up.

The neat print on the back of the gold tag read "I want you to find it again."

She knew exactly what *it* was. It meant the inexplicable feeling of magic she'd told Erik she'd once known every Christmas. The feeling of everything being right in her world. He knew it was the feeling she'd wanted her son to know and something she'd given up hope of ever experiencing again herself.

Yet that sense was what she felt now as she lifted the lid on the box to find a glittery little life preserver on a thin gold cord.

She had the feeling he was only letting her know he'd help her stay afloat with the business. And that was huge. But the way he'd done it had her closing the box and holding it with both hands to her heart.

It was only then that she looked to where Erik unfolded his arms and stepped away from his driver's side door.

Gravel crunched beneath his hiking boots as he moved past the bits of storm debris still strewn over the wet grass. Dark plaid flannel hung open over a navy Henley shirt, his broad shoulders looking impossibly wide as he climbed the steps and stopped in front of her.

He hadn't been at all sure what to expect when he'd left the box for her. He'd just wanted her to discover it the way she had the others she'd told him about. They seemed to have appeared out of nowhere, she'd said, so that sense was part of what he'd wanted to give her, even if only for a moment.

He knew he could have just left it for her. But that would have defeated another part of his purpose. He'd needed to see her reaction to his gift so he'd have some idea of what to do next. It was so unlike him not to have a clear plan, but he felt much as he suspected he would setting sail without a compass or preparation. He wasn't totally sure how to get where he wanted to go, or if the waters he'd face would be calm, rough or totally unpredictable.

Encouraged by the way she held his gift, he quietly said, "Merry Christmas."

"Merry Christmas," she echoed, still clutching the little ornament. Caution merged with disbelief. "What are you doing here? I thought you were in San Diego."

"I was. I spent Christmas Eve with my family and caught the first flight out this morning. I don't want to keep you from Tyler. I just wanted you to have that."

Rory watched him nod toward her clutched hands. She could have hugged him for his gift. The reserve carved in his expression held her right where she stood.

Considering the bated relief she felt at his presence, her "Thank you" seemed terribly inadequate. "Do you want to come in? Tyler loves his—"

Erik was already shaking his head. "There's one other thing." More than one, actually, but he wanted them alone right now. "The other day, you said you didn't want to set yourself up to lose something you don't even have. You said it would be a mistake for you to count on me. I understand the need to protect yourself," he insisted. He'd mastered that one in spades himself. "And I get the reasons you don't want Tyler to start believing I'll be around for him. But I'm not all those other people who've let you down, Rory.

"You seem so certain the only way you can create stability for yourself is to keep anyone who could rock your boat at arm's length. But you've rocked mine, too. You already have me," he admitted. "I figure the least we owe each other is a little time to reconsider our positions before we totally blow something that could have a lot of potential."

She looked at him warily, a betraying glint of a smile in her eyes. "You think we have potential?"

"Yeah," he said. "I do."

She'd rocked his boat. The thought made relief harder to suppress. His admission that she already had him made it nearly impossible.

She took a step closer. "If I let myself count on you," she began, already wanting that more than he could possibly know, "what are you offering to reconsider?"

"Are we negotiating?"

"Apparently," she replied, holding his gift even tighter.

She couldn't begin to identify what she felt as the tension left his handsome features. Reprieve, for certain. But something that felt suspiciously like hope had risen right behind it. He didn't want them to close any doors.

Lifting his hand toward her, he curved it to the side of her face.

"In that case," he said, more relieved than he could have imagined when she tipped her cheek toward his palm, "you should know I've already considered how much my hang-ups were getting in the way of possibilities where we were concerned. I've spent years thinking I just wanted to be away from here. But once I moved past thinking about what I'd wanted and considered what I might need, I realized that what I needed was another chance with you.

"You made me realize how much I still want a family. And a home here. It's not just the place," he assured her. It was how she made it feel. Comfortable. Familiar. As if he belonged there. "It's you. And Tyler."

He knew he already had a good life. Until he'd met her, he'd just refused to let it matter that he didn't have any-one to share it with. He'd work or play late so that he was too tired to care that he had no one to come home to who actually cared that he'd had a great day or a bad one, or whom he could care about in return.

"We're good together. If we want to make this work between us, we can. I'm in love with you," he confessed, finally acknowledging what he'd denied to his partner well over a week ago. Pax had somehow known that she was the woman he'd been waiting for, though he hadn't realized he'd been waiting for her at all. "All I'm asking is if you're willing to try."

Rory knew his walls had existed far longer than hers. Yet he'd just put his heart on the line for her. Her own heart feeling full enough to burst, she went up on tiptoe, curved her arms around his neck and hugged him hard.

Folding her to his chest, his hold just as tight, he chuckled against the top of her head. "That's a yes, then?"

"Absolutely."

"Are you okay?"

She nodded against his shoulder. "I'm falling in love with you, too, Erik. I think that's what scared me. I knew the day we met that it could happen, but I wasn't ready for it. It happened so fast."

Drawing a deep breath, she lowered herself to her heels and let her hands slide to his chest. Still holding the little box, she met his eyes. "I think I panicked," she explained.

He brushed back the hair the breeze fluttered across her cheek.

"I know you did." She'd been no more prepared than he'd been to put a name or label on what had seemed to be growing more complicated by the moment. A little apprehension on her part hadn't been surprising at all. He hadn't dealt with it all that fearlessly himself. "We'll take it slow now. Okay? No pressure. No rush. We'll just take our time and stay open to possibilities."

"Possibilities," Rory repeated. "That's what Phil told me I should look for here." She'd only been thinking about the property, though. As Erik smiled into her eyes and drew his hand to the back of her neck, Rory remembered that the woman had also warned her to keep an open mind about him.

"She told me that, too," he told her, and lowered his mouth to hers before she could say another word.

There was relief in his kiss as he pulled her closer, and promise, hunger, possessiveness and need. It was the need she felt most. His, definitely, but her own, too, in the long moments before he lifted his head and eased back far enough to release her hands from where they'd been trapped against his chest.

"What?" he asked, seeing the question in her flushed features.

She looked at the little gold box, lifted off its lid. Suddenly she felt certain the little life preserver didn't represent what she'd thought.

Erik's voice was quiet. "You said there was a time when you could always count on something like that being there for you Christmas morning."

Her smile came easily at the reminder. "I thought this had something to do with the store. Something about keeping it afloat. But it's a lifeline, isn't it?"

"It is," he murmured, touching his lips to her forehead. "I'm just not sure which one of us I thought needed rescuing."

"Erik!"

In a flash of maroon fleece and gray denim, Tyler bolted through the door onto the porch.

"Hey, buddy!"

"You're here!"

"I'm here," Erik agreed, and pulled him between them for a hug.

It was then that Rory felt what Erik had wanted her to glimpse again.

At that moment, all felt truly, completely and utterly right in their little world. That was the magic, and it was the most wonderful gift of all.

As they headed in from the cold, it started to snow.

Epilogue

"Why are we waiting in here, Erik?" Confusion shadowed Rory's smile. "We've said hi to Phil and Cornelia," she pointed out, their purpose at the FGI office accomplished. Or so she'd assumed.

"We'll go in a couple of minutes. This is just some of that year-end stuff I need to take care of."

He'd been busy with work off and on for the past week. That afternoon, though, he was going to show her and Tyler where he built boats.

As if anxious to get business behind him, he tugged her closer to where he stood by a gold filigree chair. "Do you want to spend tomorrow night on my houseboat? Tyler might get a kick out of the fireworks."

Tomorrow was New Year's Eve. "He'd love that. I'd love it," she stressed.

She hadn't seen his place yet, though he had warned her it was small. By land-standards, anyway.

"Then that's what we'll do."

CHRISTINE FLYNN 215

Looking more preoccupied than impatient, he glanced to the open door of the room the elegant older woman presently used as her private office. The space off the lovely conference room wasn't much bigger than a closet, but it apparently served her purpose until the major construction behind the sheets of heavy plastic in the entryway would be completed.

Beyond them, Phil and a petite, honey-gold blonde sat beneath the crystal chandelier at the mahogany table. On its surface, hundreds of letters from the mailbags mounded by the delicate French writing desk teetered in stacks. Others had been sorted into piles as the women carefully read each one.

Cornelia had introduced the pretty woman with Phil as Shea Weatherby. She was the reporter who'd written the article that had resulted in the continuing deluge of mail from prospective Cinderellas, or "Cindies," as Rory had just learned her fairy godmothers called the ladies they sponsored. She'd also just learned she'd been their second success.

As focused as Shea appeared to be on her reading, she seemed even more intent on ignoring Pax. Erik's business partner had come over with them after Erik had showed her and Tyler around their client office next door. Pax had used the excuse of needing a decent cup of coffee, something he apparently mooched off the women with some regularity. Yet it was as obvious as the charmingly devilish smile that clearly wasn't working on Shea that she was the reason he was hanging around with Tyler by the pretty little Christmas tree, checking out the boats beyond the window.

"Do you mind if I ask what we're waiting for?" Rory ventured.

"Not at all," came Erik's easy reply. "I just need to give Cornelia a check and pick up a deed from her. I'm paying off the mortgage on your property so you can stop worrying about it."

He was paying off her mortgage? "I never said I was worried."

The look he gave her said she couldn't possibly be serious. "Honey." Brushing back her bangs, he planted a kiss on the furrows between her eyes. "You've never had to tell me when you were concerned about something. I can see it. This way, the pressure's off."

"You're giving me the place?"

"Consider it a pre-engagement present."

She opened her mouth, closed it again.

"Pre-engagement?" she finally asked.

"Yeah. You know. It comes before an official engagement. If you want, I can hold off titling it to you until then. Either way, the property is yours to do with as you please."

He'd figured they could eventually live together there or he could have a bigger house built back by the woods. Whichever she wanted. With the boatworks here, he'd commute by plane most of the time. If she decided to sell or lease the place, that was her call, too. He just wanted them together. But he'd already gotten way ahead of where he figured she mentally was with their relationship.

Seeing that he'd left her a little speechless, he figured it best to change the subject. He'd told her they wouldn't rush. That they could take their time.

"Hey. Ignore me. I was just in business mode," he explained. "I hadn't intended to bring that part up until you got used to me being around." He hitched his head toward the open door. "I'm going to see what's holding up Cornelia."

He gave her a kiss, quick and hard, and turned away.

Catching his arm, she turned him right back. "I'm getting used to you," she assured him. "How long an engagement are you talking about?"

"However long you need."

Christmas morning, he'd given back to her a feeling she'd thought she'd never know again. Now he was ready to offer himself, along with the gift of time, to accept what, in her heart, she already knew.

"Then, I have no problem discussing it now." Some things, simply felt, simply were…right. "All you have to do is ask."

His eyebrow arched. "Seriously?"

"Seriously," she echoed.

With now familiar ease, he slipped his arms around her, drew her close. "In that case, I'm ready if you are."

The teasing in her expression met the smile in his. Narrowing her eyes, she tipped her head as her hands flattened on his chest. "That's a proposal?"

"It's due diligence. I don't want you to shoot me down."

"Never," she murmured. "I love you too much."

"I love you back, Rory." There'd been a time when he couldn't imagine ever saying anything like that again. Or, ever feeling what he felt with her. "And just for the record," he said, glancing toward Tyler before lowering his head to hers, "you made me believe in the magic, too."

* * * * *

Merry Christmas
& A Happy New Year!

Thank you for a wonderful
2013...

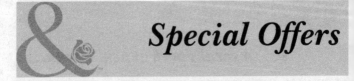

Special Offers

Every month we put together collections and longer reads written by your favourite authors.

Here are some of next month's highlights— and don't miss our fabulous discount online!

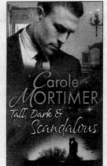

On sale 3rd January   On sale 3rd January   On sale 20th December

Save 20%
on all Special Releases

Come in from the cold this Christmas with two of
our favourite authors. Whether you're jetting off to
Vermont with Sarah Morgan or settling down for
Christmas dinner with Fiona Harper, the smiles
won't stop this festive season.

Visit:
www.millsandboon.co.uk

Join the Mills & Boon Book Club

Want to read more **Cherish**™ books?
We're offering you **2 more** absolutely **FREE!**

We'll also treat you to these fabulous extras:

- 🌹 **Exclusive offers and much more!**
- 🌹 **FREE home delivery**
- 🌹 **FREE books and gifts with our special rewards scheme**

Get your free books now!

**visit www.millsandboon.co.uk/bookclub
or call Customer Relations on 020 8288 2888**

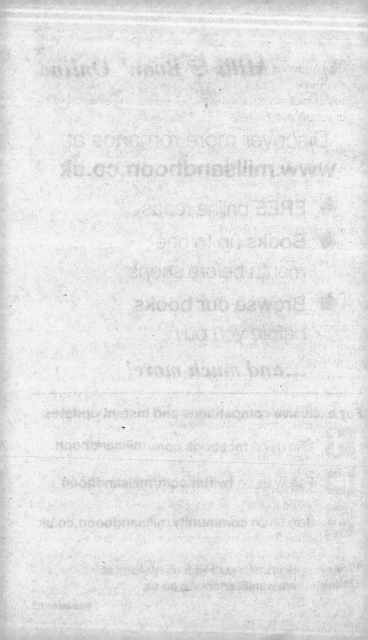